Child, Unwanted

FRIENDS IN HIGH PLACES 3:
MARGARET OF CASTELLO

CORINNA TURNER

unSeen

PRAISE FOR *CHILD, UNWANTED*

ALSO BY CORINNA TURNER:

I AM MARGARET series
For older teens and up

Brothers *(A Prequel Novella)**
1: I Am Margaret*
1: Io Sono Margaret (Italian)
2: The Three Most Wanted*
3: Liberation*
4: Bane's Eyes*
5: Margo's Diary*
6: The Siege of Reginald Hill*
7: A Saint in the Family
'The Underappreciated Virtues of Rusty Old Bicycles' *(Prequel short story) Also found in the anthology:*
Secrets: Visible & Invisible*

I Am Margaret: The Play *(Adapted by Fiorella de Maria)*

UNSPARKED series
For tweens and up

Main Series:
1: Please Don't Feed the Dinosaurs*
2: A Truly Raptor-ous Welcome
3: PANIC!*
4: Farmgirls Die in Cages*
5: Wild Life
6: A Right Rex Rodeo
7: FEAR
8: A Different Kind of Camouflage
9: A Different Kind of Freedom
10: What's Done is Done†

Prequels:
BREACH!*
A Mom With Blue Feathers†
A Very Jurassic Christmas*
'Liam and the Hunters of Lee'Vi'

FRIENDS IN HIGH PLACES series
For tweens and up

1: The Boy Who Knew (Carlo Acutis)*
2: Old Men Don't Walk to Egypt (Saint Joseph)*
3: Child, Unwanted (Margaret of Castello)*
4: A Lion for a Tomb (Ignatius of Antioch)†

Do Carpenter's Dream of Wooden Sheep? *(Spin-off, comes between 1 & 2)*

1: El Chico Que Lo Sabia (Spanish)
1: Il Ragazzo Che Sapeva (Italian)

YESTERDAY & TOMORROW series
For adults and mature teens only
Someday: A Novella*
Eines Tages (German)
1: Tomorrow's Dead†

OTHER WORKS

For teens and up
Elfling*
'The Most Expensive Alley Cat in London' *(Elfling prequel short story)*

For tweens and up
Mandy Lamb & The Full Moon*
The Wolf, The Lamb, and The Air Balloon *(Mandy Lamb novella)*

For adults and new adults
Three Last Things *or* The Hounding of Carl Jarrold, Soulless Assassin*
A Changing of the Guard
The Raven & The Yew†

† **Coming Soon**
* **Awarded the Catholic Writers Guild** *Seal of Approval*

CONTENTS

CHAPTER 1

Ahead, a plastic feed sack caught on the hedge flaps helplessly in the breeze. Stripe puts his ears back, hesitating. Shortening my reins, I keep a firm seat, allowing him a moment to look at the sack and realize it's not dangerous before giving a little squeeze with my heels, urging him on, just the way Mrs. Williams taught me.

He snorts, but his ears come forward again and he walks past the bag, making my heart swell with pride. It's so hard to believe Stripe is really mine. How can I, Miri, the most unwanted, unloved boy in the world, abandoned by *everyone* in my life, have a *pony*? Even after three weeks I can hardly believe it!

I ride on along the farm track in the bottom of the Welsh valley, the spring sun warm on my face whenever the breeze drops, the steep fields lush and green to either side. From high up the slope comes the distant purr and clank of a tractor pulling some piece of machinery. Kara mentioned that Mr. Evans was going to start baling his first cut of hay today. Mr. E's a round old gentleman, but fun.

I'd love to take Stripe over to the Williams's farm and show him off to my friends yet again, but Kara and Llewellyn made me promise not to ride across the main road by myself. They reckon I'm not an experienced enough rider yet, since I only got on a horse for the first time in my life six months ago. And they didn't break their word to me—anything but!—so I don't plan on breaking mine to them.

A year, that's what Llewellyn said. I do my chores properly for a year, and they'd buy me a pony. And three weeks ago, when I came down to breakfast during Easter week, he said I'd done my chores so well these last six months they trusted me to keep on doing them, and there was a horse fair that day, so we could go and see if there was a suitable pony. And there was Stripe!

Such a neat, sleek little pony, but I hardly noticed. One look at his face and I knew we were meant to be together. I made friends at once, and I had my arms around his neck before I noticed Kara and Llewellyn's expressions and knew that Stripe was too expensive. Oh, did my heart sink to the ground!

Even the horse trader felt sorry for me, I guess. He looked from my face to Stripe, and pulled a few faces himself, and muttered a bit. Then offered—well, I think it must've been a really good price, because Kara and

Llewellyn closed the deal, after all. And now I have a pony. A pony that looks just like me.

My hand rises, tracing the little scar over my lip, the only remaining sign of the cleft lip I was born with.

See, mother. It was so easily fixed.

My hand moves to the other scar, the one running all the way down the right side of my face, straight across my dented cheekbone, where the bone grew back together all lumpy. My dad felt really guilty about that scar, because it was him who gave my mother the money to make the failed attempt. When he was home he'd stroke it with his thumb and tell me he was saving up to get a top plastic surgeon to take the scar away completely. Soon. Soon he'd have enough.

Once he was gone again, Esme used to tell me not to get my hopes up, that it must cost most of his officer's salary to pay her and keep me. It wouldn't be any time soon, she assured me, that I'd lose that scar. Not unless Dad got promoted quite a lot.

All the same, even when I was a little older, hiding in my room, refusing-to-cry for the thousandth time because the other boys had called me Scarface and I was still too little to fight back, I used to dream. That *this time*, when Dad came home on leave, he'd tell me it was time. Instead, the day before my ninth birthday, it was an army officer and two social workers who knocked on the door, to tell us he was dead.

And the betrayal after that...

No, I refuse to think about that. My life has finally changed. Everything's going to carry on going right, now. I mean, I have a *pony*! Mrs. Williams even sent Catherine over with a bag of her cousin's old riding things yesterday. Kara was so pleased; she must've been worrying how they were going to afford things like that for me. Three pairs of jodhpurs that didn't fit half badly, and there was even a smart jacket, like Catherine and John wore at the gymkhana they took me along to.

"Good," said Kara, holding it up against my shoulders. "This will do you for a year or two. You'll need it if you want to compete."

Compete! I can see it already. There I am, wearing that smart jacket, trotting out of the ring, the announcer's voice booming behind us, "And it's a clear round! Let's have some applause for Miri and Stripe..."

Yep, my life's going to be so good, now. I'm even prepared to get confirmed—Kara and Llewellyn are keen, so I've decided to go along with it. Dad always wanted me to stop being mad at God, but I was so sure God hated me. Maybe He actually doesn't, after all— even if He did a good imitation of it, until now.

I've got to choose a confirmation saint, though. Catherine gave me a book about a Saint Margaret of Castello. I told her, no way was I having a girl's name stuck to me, but she just laughed and said lots of great male saints had taken girl's names, like Saint John Mary

Vianney and Saint Maximilian Maria Kolbe. Just like lots of girls took a boy's saint name.

And then she told me a bit about Saint Margaret. And...well, I don't reckon I'll really want a girl's name tagged on mine—mine's weird enough already, thank Esme for that. But...I am reading the book about Saint Margaret. Because nobody wanted *her*, either—her, a saint!—not for so long, maybe not ever—I haven't finished the book yet.

Sensing my inattention, Stripe ambles to a halt, stretching out his neck to grab a mouthful of hedge. Munching, he turns his head slightly, eyeing me, ears pricked, giving me a clear look at the very thin white blaze that runs down the right side of his face, weirdly off-center. Catherine says he's clearly been beautifully trained but not given much affection. I love him and I don't care who knows it—and he already loves me right back.

Yeah, Kara and Llewellyn would be disappointed if they saw me getting this distracted while riding. They said I can ride by myself on the farm track through the fields, on past Mr. E's farm, no roads, so long as I'm careful. I've got the Saint Margaret book with me, so I can tie Stripe to the tree by the stream when I reach the glade and read for a while.

"Okay," I tell Stripe—and them, though they're back up at the farmhouse. "I'm paying attention. Come on, let's go, walk on..."

Kara and Llewellyn. It's so hard to even think about my hope after what Esme— No. Not going there. I dismissed what they said totally, when I first arrived. I mean, me? Come on. Who is going to want *me*? They just wanted to get paid to have a healthy thirteen-year-old boy around to do chores on their struggling hill farm, right? 'Marginally viable' means 'struggling,' right?

But...they bought me a pony. They kept their word. And they've said... They've told me, straight out, what they intend. Will they keep their word again? Will they really...adopt me?

I can still hardly bring myself to even think it. But...they bought me Stripe.

I pat his neck and try to concentrate again. They will or they won't. I'm being good, haven't fought with anyone since I got here, there's nothing more I can do than that, is there?

Stripe stops, ears flicking, snorting. What? There's a strange noise, a clanking-revving- crashing-undulating, louder and louder and —

I look around. A red tractor and hay baler is rolling — rolling side over side, like a rolling pin! — down the hill straight towards me. Time seems to slow — I start to press my heels to Stripe — the tractor bounces, smashing through the last hedge —

Stripe rears up —

And it hits.

CHAPTER 2

I'm five years old and I'm sitting on Esme's lap, crying.

Scarface. Scarface. Scarface. The words still echo in my ears.

"Oh, hush," she tells me. "You must learn not to let it get to you. It's not your fault, the way you look, but you can't change it. Your face is scarred, you know. But that scar saved your life."

"But..." I sniff even harder, desperate to make her understand. "But...they say it so... They're nasty."

She hugs me. "Yes, they're nasty. But you must get used to it. Don't let it get under your skin. It's not your fault."

"Whose fault is it?"

"Why, it's the abortionist's fault. And your mother for taking you there to have it done. And your father for paying for it. Haven't I told you the story?"

I've heard little bits and pieces, but I still can't fit it all together. It makes it feel like beetles are crawling in my stomach, to think that Dad… "Tell me again! Tell me how this scar saved my life?"

"Well," Esme sits up straighter, the way she does when she tells stories, especially ones with her in them, "I was working as a midwife in the hospital. Your mother had received a late diagnosis of cleft lip. She'd been very much in two minds about the pregnancy from the beginning, to hear your father tell it, so that was the final straw, I suppose. She demanded your father pay for an abortion, on grounds of fetal abnormality.

"Because it was later than usual in the pregnancy, she came to the hospital to have it done, rather than at a clinic. And the doctor was in the midst of a full-blown nervous breakdown, though no one had cottoned on yet. And he messed it up. Put the scissors through your cheekbone instead of your skull and then, because you were so small, he just pulled you straight out without doing anything more. Dumped you in the corner to stop twitching and off he went to his next patient, never realizing what he'd done.

"Well, I was a young and inexperienced midwife. If I'd known— Well, anyway, I saw you were alive—bleeding but alive—and I couldn't just ignore you. I picked you up and took you out of the room and quietly put you in a bassinet and wheeled you into the premature baby unit; murmured something about an accident during delivery. They took over immediately and gave you the very best care and, you know, it took them several days to figure out who you were and where you'd come from. And by that time even the most pro-choice among them couldn't stomach pulling the plug on you, though they were very uncomfortable about your existence. So they kept treating you and you survived. It really was a miracle, that you survived all that. That's why I called you that, little Miracle."

She strokes my cheek gently with her thumb, but I never like it when she does that, because her brow wrinkles as she does it, not like when Dad strokes my scar. He only looks sad. I want to twist away, but I don't want to stop the story.

"What happened then?"

"Well, your mother was absolutely furious when they contacted her. Insisted she wanted nothing to do with you and that you were to be put into state care. But your father felt bad and decided to take responsibility for you himself. That was the final straw with his relationship with your mother and she broke things off completely. Then she threatened to sue the hospital for botching the abortion so badly and they found some excuse to fire me to get her off their back. They fired me so badly my career was over."

"But Dad hired you!" I know this bit.

"Yes, your father felt bad about that too and hired me. He was away too much to raise a baby, after all. So now I look after you. All those years of midwifery training and— But you are a very precious boy, Miri. Do you understand how that scar saved your life?"

The doctor cut my cheekbone instead of my skull... "Are skulls more important than cheekbones?"

"Yes, Miri. Far more important."

+

I can't breathe properly. Something is crushing my chest, filling my throat. I want to scream and struggle, but I can't even twitch. I can't move at all. I hurt all over, but kind of dimly, like I'm feeling the pain through water. Or something...

+

I still can't breathe. What's happening to me? I can hear. Beeping. A soft, rhythmic hiss. Occasional distant rattling sounds. Murmurs of passing voices. But I'm too tired to open my eyes...

+

If only I could get this elephant off my chest. And whatever it is that's wedged all down my throat. It feels *horrible*. Is it a snake? An alien? Panic flashes through me, dimming the pain, dimming...

+

I can see! This time, as I woke, I managed to open one eye. Ugly square roof tiles waver high above me. To the left I glimpse one of those IV bag things you see on hospital TV shows. I'm in hospital! I haven't been abducted by aliens or locked in a room full of snakes or...

Why am I in hospital? I struggle to remember, but thinking hurts as much as everything else and before long I sink into a numb mental silence.

Eventually, footsteps enter the room. A few clanks, as though of furniture moving, soft sweeping sounds.

Two male voices begin to talk to one another.

"I mean, this one is a perfect example of what I was saying. Why the heck are they trying so hard to save him?"

"It's their job, stupid."

"But it's not helping him. What sort of life is this kid gonna have, now? They should've just let him go."

"Come on, man, think of his parents!"

"He hasn't even got any. That woman hanging around is just a foster-carer, right?"

"He's a real fighter. I heard Dr. Yazmani say so. Or he'd be dead."

"So his body doesn't know what's best for it. See, that's precisely what I'm saying. In this sort of case, they should just give them, y'know, an injection or something. For their own good."

"That's messed up, man. You shouldn't talk like that."

"If he was a dog, no one would make him live like that."

"He's not a dog. That's the point."

"No, *you're* missing the point..."

Their footsteps dwindle and so do their voices. I can't pant in terror because I can't control my breathing—the elephant on my chest and the snake in my throat are in control of that. I lie, fear sparking around my fuzzy mind like little flashes of electricity. *Injection... Let him go...* Are they going to...are they going to, like, abort me, finish the job, now, after all this time? Are they gonna...

No! No, I don't want to die! I don't...

Don't let them...

I've got to...got to stay awake. Got to stay awake in case they come to...to abort me. Got to...stay...awake...

Help...please...

CHAPTER 3

I drag my working eye open again, peering at the square-tiled ceiling. I'm still alive. No one has 'let me go' yet. Panic still sputters around inside me, though, flaring up as a shuffling noise comes from the doorway. But it's just a little old lady, tiny and deeply bent over, shuffling towards the bed, using a crutch to walk. She must have the wrong room.

Walking looks such hard work for her, I want to save her the trouble. "I think you've come to the wrong room," I tell her.

She looks up. Oh. She's *not* old. She's really ugly, but she's not old at all. Her face looks no older than Kara's. Just...a *lot* less pretty. Her weather-beaten skin is a very light brown, and she looks a bit...Spanish? Italian? A simple white dress is gathered in at the waist by a leather belt, and she wears a white bandanna on her head. Her eyes don't seem to focus on me.

"Are you Miri?" Her voice is sweet and gentle. So sweet and gentle I'd assume she was putting it on, except somehow I know she isn't.

"Oh. Yeah, I'm Miri."

"It's you I've come to visit."

"Really?"

"*Si.*"

"What language is that?"

"It's Italian for yes."

Awkwardly, she wriggles up onto the chair by the bed, clearly designed for a much taller person than she is, and arranges her crutch neatly against the arm rest.

"I don't mean to be rude but..." I hesitate, "I don't know you. Why are you here to see me?"

"I visit many sick people. And we have met, sort of."

Have we? I must've been very young or I'd definitely remember. I mean...I eye the strange little lady as well as I can with only one eye open. She's *so* ugly and crippled. I'd be super embarrassed to walk into school with her and announce she was my friend. But who am I to call her ugly? Me, Scarface? And she seems ever so sweet and nice. So I just say, "Uh, are you from Italy?"

"I am."

"Have you always been..." I flick my gaze up and down her twisted body before realizing my question's probably rather rude.

But she just smiles that sweet smile, still not quite looking right at me. "Oh yes. I was born this way."

Born that way. "And your parents didn't mind? You lucky thing! My mum wasn't even prepared to put up with my cleft lip, when the prenatal scan came back."

The lady smiles. "There weren't any prenatal scans in Italy in 1287."

"Oh." Something about what she just said seems slightly odd, but I can't figure it out.

"Tragically, my parents," she goes on, "were expecting a perfect, first-born boy. Instead, out I came, female, hunchbacked, lame, and a dwarf. They had two huge parties planned, you know. My father, whose Christian name was Parisio—my mother's name was Emilia, but forgive me if I do not tell you my family name—had won a famous victory and had become commander of the great fortress of Metola long before I was conceived. They were going to have one party at the fortress and a second one at their *palazzo* in the town. All very grand. I remember the servants and soldiers and serfs telling me about the lost party when I was a little girl. They were all so disappointed when it was cancelled. There would have been venison and game and jugglers and sweetmeats and such treats as they'd scarcely ever had in their lives."

"And it was cancelled? Just because you were... um...a bit disabled?"

The little lady laughs. "You are such a polite boy. A total cripple, my father always said. Me, I never thought so. When I was little, there was a soldier's mother who lay paralyzed in a little chamber off the barracks for almost five years, unable to leave her bed at all. I would often go in and visit her, and how grateful I was that *I* could go around on my own two feet, with a little help from my wooden friend." Her hand moves to touch the crutch handle beside her.

"I suppose when you look at it that way..."

"Oh, I had a blessed childhood. A busy castle is a lovely place for a child to grow up, even a blind one. I knew my way everywhere."

I focus on her eyes. No, she still hasn't looked at me, not properly. "You're blind, too?"

She nods. "I think that was the last straw for my parents, when they realized. Though it pains me to speak ill of them, the truth is, they were deeply ashamed of me and did not wish to be reminded of my existence. The one place in the castle I never went was their apartment." Her voice is sad, but still so gentle.

My mother, still alive somewhere but wanting nothing to do with me, fills my mind. And Esme... It makes me feel anything but gentle. "Yeah? I know how that feels. *Blessed childhood?* Weren't you miserable?"

She shakes her head. "No, for I was friends with virtually everyone else in the castle, and there were many sick and elderly folk for me to visit. Any free moments could be spent in the chapel, in the best company of all. And the chaplain, dear, good Fra Giacomo Cappellano, took an interest in me from an early age. It was he who persuaded my parents to let a maid take me anonymously to the cathedral in the big town to have me baptized, to my eternal gratitude! It was the maid who chose my name."

"Not your parents?" I feel a surge of excited kinship with her. "Why, my parents didn't choose my name, either. My nurse did! She called me Miracle. What did the maid call you?"

"Margaret. It means 'Pearl,' as Fra Cappellano told me as I grew older and better able to understand things. Such a beautiful name. Have you heard of the 'pearl of great price'?"

"Uh..." My mind skitters back seven or eight years, to sitting on Dad's knee one Sunday when he was home. "Um, it's from the Bible, right?"

"Yes. Fra Cappellano took the time to teach me the catechism, even though I could not read or write. He spoke in such glowing terms of my intelligence to my parents, it makes me blush even now. I am sure he exaggerated, dear man, seeking to compensate for my physical lacks."

Her blind eyes turn modestly downwards as she speaks, her dainty hands clasped elegantly in her lap. Despite all the hunched crookedness of her body, she truly carries herself like a lady. Daughter of a great house, huh? Well, that's something we don't have in common. Miracle Taylor is the son of nobody in particular. Well, at the funeral, his commanding officer said my dad was a 'very clever man' which always struck me as weird, but then, no one ever would tell me exactly what Dad *did* in the army that kept him away from home so much of the time. 'Brave' or 'strong' or 'a good shot' would've made more sense. But 'clever'?

"Do you remember the story?" she asks. "About the pearl, my namesake?"

"Um. There was a field in it?"

"Yes, there is a field in it. Would you like to hear it?"

"Um...yes?" I'm not wildly interested in Bible stories, but I'm enjoying her visit more than I would have expected. I love the bright sparkle of her unfocussed eyes, her gentle voice, and the way all her attention seems to be on boring me, despite her blindness.

"Well, once there was a merchant..."

+

Margaret is gone when I wake again. I must have nodded off while she was telling the story, though I remember most of it. The man sold all the less valuable things he owned—every last one—to buy one thing of supreme importance—the field in which a priceless pearl was hidden. All about getting your priorities straight, Margaret said the story was.

But as I slowly come fully awake, I remember my danger and fear grows again. Why didn't I tell Margaret about the men, ask for help? How could I be so stupid?

I drag open the one eye that responds and try to see around the room. The snake remains lodged in my throat. The elephant still presses on my chest, up, down, up, down. Maybe it's got its trunk down my throat, breathing into me. *In. Out.* That would make sense. I try to move a hand, a finger, anything, but I can barely feel them. I'm helpless in a vague sea of pain. Oh, why didn't I ask Margaret for help?

Margaret, come back. I try to whisper it, but I can't even draw in a breath. *Hiss. Hiss. Hiss.* The elephant breathes when it chooses. Fear and frustration overwhelm me so much that I feel a drop of liquid trickle down my face from my eye. Not a tear, of course. Miracle Taylor never cries.

"Miri?" Kara's face appears over mine, so pretty compared to Margaret's, yet lacking that bizarre radiance. Her sudden appearance still makes me think of angels from heaven. Her finger touches my face, wiping the liquid away. "Oh, Miri, are you awake?" She leans close to kiss my forehead.

I've got to speak to her, tell her I don't want to be aborted. *Yes, I'm moving my lips!* But I still can't get control of any air to speak...

"Oh, no, Miri, don't try to talk! Don't try to talk, lamb. You're on a ventilator. That's what the tube in your throat is. It's doing your breathing for you, to help you heal. It's doing you a lot of good, but you can't speak. I know it must be horribly uncomfortable, frightening, even, but they will take it out as soon as they can, I promise. Can you understand me? Blink once if you understand me?"

I blink once. A big smile covers her face, along with an intensity of relief in her eyes that frightens me more than anything she's said. Ventilator... Only really sick people get put on ventilators. But she said they'll take it out soon, right? But how do I tell her there are abortionists here, threatening to kill me?

I blink once. I pause, then blink twice. Once again. Then twice.

"Miri? What are you doing?" She isn't stupid and, thank God, she catches on quickly. "Do you want to tell me something? Oh, um...okay, I'll go through the alphabet, okay? Blink when I get to the right letter. Hang on..."

After she's hastily dug out a piece of paper and a pen from her handbag, I painstakingly spell out:

DONTLETKILLME

She stares at what she's written down, her eyes widening.

"No one is going to *kill* you, Miri! Heavens above! Where did you get such an idea? You're in a top children's hospital in London and the doctors are doing everything they can, and...and you're coming on very well. I've been right here almost the whole time. Don't try to turn your head, but there's a little couch against the wall over there. I've been sleeping on that."

She has? What about the farm? Where's Llewellyn?

"Llewey's at home," she says, as though reading my mind, "looking after the livestock. He's coming over at the weekend, though, when his brother can hold down the fort for a few days. Llewellyn wants so much to be here too."

She sounds like she really means it. I suppose a thousand sheep, sixty cows, fifteen hens, five dogs, two cats, and one pony can't just be left totally unattended.

One pony. What is it about that thought that puts my guts into a blender?

I'm not sure. It's just so hard to think straight...

"It's okay, Miri." Kara strokes my forehead gently, or at least the left side of my forehead, over my working eye. "You're on a lot of morphine and painkillers. If your thoughts feel all jumbled, that's why. You might even see something odd, like pigs flying past the window or crazy stuff like that. Don't worry about it. It's not real, okay? You don't need to do anything right now but relax and rest and get better."

Okay? Is everything okay? I'm not sure. I'm not sure at all, but I feel so...

CHAPTER 4

Margaret's there again when I wake. I smile at her and she smiles back, as though she can sense my smile somehow.

"So, when you got older," I ask, trying to sound casual, "did your parents like you better?" I still entertain this fantasy, only in weak moments, that my mum will totally change her mind and come for me. Or even that Esme might relent. "Was there anything you did that helped?"

Margaret smiles her sad smile. "I'm sorry, Miri. My parents never changed their minds about me. In fact, things got worse, if truth be told."

"Worse?" Than completely ignoring a little girl?

"Yes. When I was six years old and still too innocent to fully understand how my parents felt about me, visitors came one day but my nurse forgot to tell me to stay in my room. So I met a stranger in the corridors, a lady, and spoke to her for a while, which I enjoyed very much, though little did I know what price I would pay for the novelty. My nurse did find me just before I could reveal my parentage, but it was a very near-thing and it frightened my father to death. He could not abide the thought of anyone knowing about me."

"So he put you into care?"

"Would that he had. In thirteenth-century Italy, the closest thing to putting me into care for a man of his rank would have been to place me in a convent with a modest dowry for my upkeep, which would have suited me very well. Plenty of friends and plenty of prayer. But no. Unfortunately, Fra Cappellano, the chaplain, had just recently narrated to Mother and Father the story of Saint Veridiana, who was what used to be known as a recluse or 'anchoress.'"

"I don't know what that is," I admit.

"Why would you? They barely exist anymore. They are somewhat like a hermit, only their isolation is more rigidly enforced, though voluntarily chosen, and tied to one particular place. An anchorite or anchoress was a man or woman who chose to be sealed up in a small cell for life to devote him or herself to prayer and fasting. An anchor of holiness in the stormy seas of the world."

"Wow. That's..." I pause, floundering for a word. Grim? Extreme? Dedicated? If they *choose* to do it... "Impressive," I manage, at last. "But weird."

Margaret's radiant smile flashes again. "Indeed.

Even back then it was deemed extreme. But the holy choice of Saint Veridiana allowed my father to believe that it was an acceptable choice to make for a young girl of six years old."

"What? Wait, he *what?*"

"He had a stone cell built alongside a remote little church out in the forest and sealed me up inside it. He intended to leave me there for my entire life, so no one would ever see me."

I splutter, too outraged to speak.

"I admit," Margaret said quietly, "that first night, all alone in the cold, listening to the wolves howling in the distance, I felt very frightened and alone. I would have given anything to be back in the castle, sleeping in my little bed with my nurse nearby, waking up to visit the old folk in the morning, going out to play with the castle children and walking in the sun in the sweet-smelling herb garden in the afternoon. I'd had a blessed life up until then and, even so young, I appreciated what I had lost. So I did feel very sad, and I even wept a little in pity for myself, those first few nights."

"I don't blame you!" I say. Not that I would have *wept*, of course, because Miracle Taylor never cries.

"But thanks to the—" Margaret pauses, and I can see her searching for a kind word "—thanks to the *honesty* of my parents, I already knew how unlike other children I was. I already knew I was ugly and hunchbacked and lame and crippled, a blind dwarf who could never hope to marry or raise a family or run a home of my own—"

"That's a load of *rubbish!*" I explode. "There's no reason you can't marry or have a family or a home—"

"Ah, Miri, you are very sweet. Times have changed, you are right. There is no reason now why a cripple may not do those things, in some parts of the world, at least. But at that time, what my parents had told me was perfectly correct. There was no possibility of any of that. So, despite my age, I had already had reason to think a great deal about pearls and fields, you understand. I had not reasoned it all through in a complicated way, of course, but at a fundamental level, I *understood.*"

"Understood what?"

"The purpose of my life. Of anyone's life."

"Purpose?" I frown. *Purpose* of life? What is the purpose of life? Having a good time, maybe? A good career? No. Having people who care about you, surely that's more important? Yeah, no wonder my life is so rubbish.

"The purpose of life," Margaret says softly, "is to love God as much as one possibly can."

I frown at her. "Is that all?"

"All?" She laughs at me, but so gently I don't mind. "God is the perfection of truth, and of beauty, and of love. All those things, to the greatest degree you can imagine and then infinitely more. Do you know what infinite means?"

"Of course!"

"Then how can so infinite a calling as loving infinite truth, beauty, and love ever warrant an 'is that all'?"

I mull that over for a while. I suppose I'm not used to thinking of God as important. It's like, if he's mentioned, I just assume the thing *isn't* that important. But Margaret's words burrow into my brain.

Infinite.

Love. Everyone knows love is important. I just can't seem to get any.

Beauty. I *hate* beauty. Beauty's why everyone hates *me.*

Truth...

"Miri?" I jerk fully awake with a start. Kara is bending over me. "Oh, you are awake." A smile makes her face even prettier, such a contrast with Margaret's, yet oddly both are attractive in their own way. "I wasn't sure."

I try to return her smile around the elephant's trunk—ventilator—making her smile even more. "Oh Miri, it's so nice to see you improving. You've been really out of it."

Have I? She must mean longer ago, because Margaret was just here. My new, strange little friend.

"Llewey's still all set for the weekend," she's telling me. "He can't wait to see you. When I told him you were properly awake and we'd even had a little conversation, he practically broke down."

Really? I try to picture my tough, sinewy, dark-haired Welsh foster-father that overcome. Difficult. And about *me*? Harder still. But then, they did buy me a...

Stripe.

Stripe! What the— My heart rate kicks up, pounding painfully in my chest. *A red tractor, rolling, bouncing*— I try to cry out, but my lips just ripple soundlessly.

"Miri, are you okay?"

Stripe!

I blink at Kara, rapidly. *Get your paper out, come on...*

"What... Do you want to talk again? Hang on..." A second later, I glimpse a notepad in her hands. She must've had it ready nearby. "Okay, Miri, let's go. A, B, C..."

STRIPE

Her face tenses, closes, as the word takes shape. Looking up at her as I am, I have a good view of the tension in her neck as she swallows several times. Dread gathers inside me, building in my chest like fizzy bubbles in a pop bottle.

"Uh, Miri, lamb, maybe you should just rest and...and not worry about anything right now..."

I blink furiously at her until she lets out a big sigh.

"Oh, Miri, I didn't want to tell you until you were feeling better. I'm so sorry, but...we couldn't save Stripe.

He was too badly hurt. I'm *so* sorry, Miri."

Heat pricks my eye, burns up my jam-packed throat. Stripe... My perfect pony twin. He's...gone. I only had three weeks with him. God *must* hate me. Why else would he give me Stripe and then take him away like this?

"He...he was such a brave little pony," Kara goes on, her voice shaking. "The accident investigator said he must've reared up, trying to protect you, maybe, and so he took the worst of the impact. Probably saved your life. But then, of course, he came down on top of you as well and— Oh, Miri, I'm sorry. He was such a good little pony."

Stripe saved my life? My eye burns worse and worse, but I refuse to blink or let any tears out. Did God give me Stripe to save my life? Or is He just playing with me? What's good and beautiful about this? As for true—well, dead is truth, I guess. Like Dad. Utter, merciless truth.

I want to turn my head away, but I still can't move. I close my eyelid instead. Yeah, what's wrong with my other eye? Why does it seem glued shut? That whole side of my face is one of the parts of me that hurts the most. That and my hands. And everything from the waist down.

But I don't really care right now. Stripe is dead. I'm just Miri the unwanted again, alone and friendless and worthless. My perfect pony twin...

I keep my eye closed tight, because it's watering badly. Something must've got in it.

CHAPTER 5

It's only when I hear the shuffle of Margaret's twisted feet and the tap of her crutches that I realize I'm not totally friendless any more. She settles in the chair, smiling. I want to pour my heart out about Stripe, but then I remember how she just told me that her own father walled her up in a little stone cell when she was six years old, and suddenly I'm afraid she'll think I'm insensitive, fretting about a mere pony. I mean, people weren't so worried about animals in the old days, right?

"How did you escape from the cell?" I ask her, instead. Maybe listening to her story will take my mind off how miserable I feel about Stripe without me needing to mention him.

"I didn't," she says simply. "My father put me in there and nobody dared to protest, not even his knights. Only Fra Cappellano, the chaplain, usually so timid with my father, dared confront him about what he had done. I'm afraid he even called the wrath of God down on my parents, but they didn't pay any attention even to that."

"Serves them right," I say, but Margaret just gives her head a sad shake, silently chiding me.

"The chaplain was allowed to visit me, though," she continues, "which was a great comfort. For a time it quite overwhelmed me to think that God thought me worthy to imitate Him so closely, suffering rejection just as Jesus had done, for I was not at all good enough for such a gift. But I decided to do all I *could* do to make myself worthy. If I was to be an anchoress, I would be the best one I could be."

"How?" I ask.

"I took on a strict regime of fasting and devoted the majority of my time to prayer. I even had the direct presence of the Blessed Sacrament in the neighboring church, through a hagioscope—" she sees my blank look and smiles "—sorry, a 'squint' or little peephole, thoughtfully built into my anchorhold—cell—so that I could adore His unseen Presence day or night. I also wore a hair shirt, though I was always afraid my mother might notice its bulk under my clothes when she visited."

"She did visit you, then?" I've never even *met* my mother.

"Just occasionally, yes. I always felt sad when she left. But then I would think how grateful I was that she came at all and my happiness returned."

Heck, even locked up, she saw more of her mother than I ever have!

"Were you happy, then, living in there?" It's hard to imagine, a six-year-old living alone like that.

"That's a difficult question. There are different kinds of happiness. Physically, it was difficult—winter was an agony of cold and summer a long torment of heat—yet the pleasure I took in the gentle warmth of spring and the mildness of autumn was far keener than I'd ever felt while living inside a comfortable castle. I missed the society of people, yet I was able to live in an intimacy with God that would have been impossible were He not my first and, most of the time, my only, Companion."

"And then," she turns her face down but speaks frankly, "when I became a teenager, I became aware that my nature was so passionate I might have been exposed to extreme temptations had I not been safe within my walls and, indeed, to remain virtuous was a greater happiness than any fleeting pleasure could bring me."

She raises her head again. "So although it would be a lie to say I did not suffer extremely during those thirteen years, both physically and emotionally, in a way I was very happy."

"Thirteen years? That's terrible."

"Oh, that prison was not so terrible and once I had

set myself to live the life of an anchoress I did not even think of it as such. I could hear the beautiful song of the birds and the bubble of the brooks and the wind in the trees, like little whispers from the tongue of God. But when I was eighteen, Massa Trabaria—my state—was invaded by the neighboring state of Urbino. My father was Captain of the People and it was his duty to lead the defense. The day I heard the church bells ringing, warning of the invasion, I wept with fear for him and prayed harder than ever."

"Fear? I'd have thought you'd be all too happy for him to get run through, if it meant you could be free at last."

I get another sad look. "Is that how you feel, then, about your mother and Esme?"

For a moment, her words strike me dumb. Because I don't, do I? However angry I feel...I don't actually want them *dead*. I mean, if they were dead...all hope would be gone. Not that my hope is *real*, really, and I kind of hate myself for it. "They haven't got me locked up, though," I point out defensively.

"Haven't they?" she speaks very softly, then continues, "My father moved my mother to their *palazzo* in the town of Mercatello for safety and, fearing I would be discovered by the enemy scouts, he took me there as well. I was shut in the vaults under the *palazzo*, and I admit they were very dark days for me.

"You see, at Metola, the chaplain knew about me,

and my father allowed him to say Mass in the church that my cell was built against—my precious peephole gave me direct access to the altar, even though I could not see it—and he often brought me the sacraments of Penance and the Eucharist. But in Mercatello my father forbade any priest to be told of my existence. I spent my days without the spiritual consolations to which I was accustomed, in fear for my father and in sorrow at the horrors of war that were ravaging my country and claiming so many lives."

"Well, that's grim," I say. "What happened?"

"Thankfully, my father, for all his cruelt—that is, for all his firmness, was indeed a very skilled general. When he put up a strong initial defense of the state, men flocked to his banner and soon he turned the tables and invaded Urbino instead. Malatesta also invaded Urbino, from the north, leaving them with a war on two fronts. Well, as you can imagine, they soon made peace. My father came home safely and more of a national hero than ever."

"Well, that's good, I suppose," I say grudgingly, since she looks so happy about it. Is there a resentful bone in her twisted little body?

"Fra Cappellano had been my greatest friend at Metola, along with Our Lord in the Blessed Sacrament." Something about the way she says it makes me think she knows about Stripe already. "It was a terrible blow to lose both my dear friends when I was locked in the crypt. I felt as though I was suffering a direct assault from the evil one."

"What do you mean?" The evil one? The devil? That's something I've never thought about before. Maybe the devil killed Stripe, not God.

"Well," she leans forward a little, speaking very earnestly, "the evil one, you see, wants nothing so much as to separate us from God. When something bad happens to us, whether the evil one is the direct cause or indirect cause or it is just natural chance, the evil one is still in there like a shot, trying to use that misfortune to turn us against God. Whispering to us, goading us. A misfortune by itself is of no account, if we turn it to good, I wish more people understood that. But if we allow it to draw us away from God, then it truly is a very grave misfortune indeed."

I frown, trying to get my head around what she's saying. I've never been interested in this sort of...of moral lecture, but Margaret speaks with such conviction and as though she deeply cares about me. As though what she's saying is deeply important to me. Losing Stripe is a misfortune, as she puts it, no question. And I immediately got mad at God about it. Am I letting the evil one win?

"But why does God let bad things happen?" I ask her.

She gives a sad smile. "A vast question, Miri. But I have always believed that a thing can be considered bad or good only according to its final result, rather than its superficial appearance. Look at me. I was born crippled and blind. Most would say that was bad, but it helped me so much in drawing closer to God that I consider it a great gift."

Gift? I stare at her, at her ugly, radiant, sincere face. "Do you really mean that?"

"Yes. I always did and I always will."

CHAPTER 6

Earlier this morning, they removed the ventilator. I still feel weak as a kitten, but it turns out my complete inability to move was partly caused by the drugs they were giving me to make sure I wouldn't fight the ventilator and hurt myself. My throat aches, but I'm feeling a bit more alert. I shift my head, trying to see down my body. The blankets stick up oddly over my feet and hands and waist.

"What's under there?" I rasp.

"Shhhh," Kara soothes me. "It's better if you don't talk too much today. Let your throat heal. And, uh, don't try to move your arms or legs, okay?"

"What's under there?" It comes out even raspier.

She sighs, stroking the hair on the left side of my head. Always the left. The right side of my face seems to be plastered in something, covering my eye and cheek and ear completely.

"They had to put some pins in to hold some of your bones together because they were badly broken. They can remove them once you've healed up enough."

Some pins? I peer at the lumpy blankets. What the heck? "How bad?" Talking really does hurt.

"It's too soon for them to say exactly, Miri." She speaks would-be-casually, but I recognize adult evasion when I hear it.

Heck. How bad *am* I hurt?

"What's wrong...face?"

Kara hesitates, then seems to realize that if she doesn't answer I'll just say it all over again, more painful each time. "It got gashed by a baler tine. And, uh, burned a bit."

"Burned?"

"Yes." She swallows. "The...the tractor caught fire, you see. You were still under the baler and Str... You were under the baler. We got to you almost in time, pulled you clear. But a bit of diesel or oil had splashed on your face during the accident. Actually—" she clenches her shaking hands together "—actually, it was something of a miracle the tractor did catch fire. Diesel, you know—they don't catch light like petrol vehicles."

Miracle? She notices my astonished stare and hurries on, "Because we saw the smoke from the farmhouse and rushed down there. If it hadn't caught fire, we wouldn't have missed you for hours, would we? And...well, it would have been too late by then. The fire saved your life. Although...although it did burn your face a...a little."

From her quivering lip and all those dressings... maybe a lot. I draw in a huge breath down my aching throat and stare up at the ceiling tiles. Great. Just *great*. What will they call me now? *Double* Scarface? Then again, I don't go to school any more...

"I'm not going to school?" I stare at Llewellyn when he drops the bombshell on my second morning at the farm. "Seriously?"

"Yep. Our neighbors have been homeschooling for years and they've been good enough to say you can join them. We think we'll give it a try for a while. You might do better if there are less people for you to fight with."

"I'll only do better if there are less people who need fighting with!" I snap.

Llewellyn just smiles. "I think the Williamses can supply that, too."

...Y'know, I don't think Catherine, John, and Paul *will* be mean about some more scars on my face. I mean, Paul asked all sorts of honest kid questions about my scar so I suppose he'll do that again, because he's only seven, but John, who's ten, and Catherine, who's fifteen, just ignore it, like it doesn't matter to them.

My mind goes back to the tractor. It caught fire... that's bad...but the result was that it saved my life... that's good. "Like what Margaret said," I croak.

"Who's that, lamb?"

Kara can't have met Margaret around the hospital yet or she wouldn't have to ask. How many teeny-weeny Italian ladies with crutches do you see around? I can't explain now, it will hurt too much. I smile with the uncovered side of my face and say nothing more. Kara smiles in relief and strokes my hair, on and on, as though she's determine to lull me to...to sleep...

Something about the tractor is bothering me. But I'm so...tired...

+

"Mr. Evans!" It comes to me as I wake from an uneasy doze.

Over on the couch, Kara sits up with a jerk, blinking. "Hmm? Miri?"

"That was Mr. E's tractor! Is he okay?" Our closest neighbor after the Williamses, a cheerful old gentleman, quite posh, he reminds me a lot of Dad's commanding officer. He was even in the army, years ago—he told me so.

"So, this is the valley's very own Miracle," he boomed, the first time he met me. "Well, young Miri, come apple-time, you help yourself from my orchard any time you like. There shall be no talk of scrumping, none. A growing boy needs a good supply of apples."

He's loud, but kind, and takes my scarred face completely in his stride.

Kara comes to the bed and settles into the chair.

"Mr. Evans?" I ask yet again, but her face is all

drawn and serious.

"Miri..." She strokes my accessible bit of forehead. "The accident happened because Mr. Evans had a heart attack while he was baling his hay. The tractor went out of control and rolled. The medical examiner and the investigator—well, they're pretty certain he was already dead by the time it hit you. Certainly by the time— I'm just saying, it was very quick, he didn't suffer. But...he is dead, Miri. I'm sorry."

I suppose I knew that already, from her face. I stare up at the ceiling. Stripe *and* Mr. Evans. I can't help remember what Margaret said about the soldier's old paralyzed mother and herself. I mean, Stripe and Mr. E are both *dead*. I'm just a bit...knocked about. Okay, more than a bit. But I am alive. Maybe I should count my blessings.

How knocked about?

"Can I see?"

Kara focuses on my eye. "See what?"

"Under the blankets."

A...scared...look enters her eyes. "Oh, I don't think that would be helpful, Miri. The pins are only temporary. Don't worry about them."

"I want to see. I want to know why it's so important I don't move my arms or legs."

"You're got broken bones, lamb," she says gently. "Broken bones in all those places. You just need to stay still and let them heal."

"I want to see!"

"Oh, Miri..."

"Let me see, or I'll try to move them myself!"

"No! Miri, don't be rash. Just stay still. Alright, I'll lift the blanket. But the pins are only temporary, okay?"

She takes hold of the blanket and carefully lifts it. Raising my head enough to peep is exhausting. Pain spikes in my burned cheek and neck but I grit my teeth and keep my head up.

It takes a while to make sense of what I'm seeing. I look like...I look like a mutant robot's giant pincushion. It's horrible. There are metal pins coming out of me everywhere. My arms are strapped to arm-shaped boards. More pins...

A scream wrenches hoarsely from me, and Kara drops the blanket at once.

"Oh, Miri. It's okay, Miri. Just temporary. Please don't worry. You just need to rest..."

I thrash my head from side to side, wanting to escape, escape from the sight, escape from the beeping, the scents, the sounds... I look like a mad scientist's project, like a...a...

Running footsteps...a nurse appears, holding a syringe. She slides the needle into my arm...

Wait...an injection...are they aborting me? Because I'm...I'm making a fuss...

"No!" I scream. "No, don't. Don't kill me! Please!"

"It's alright, Miri! It's alright!" Kara's holding me

down gently, tears running down her cheeks, while the nurse messes with the little machine.

"It's okay," she says to Kara. "He'll settle off to sleep now. And I raised his painkillers a little."

I want...I just want...my throat burns from my rapid breaths. Burns... Did Mr. E burn? Kara said not... I hope not... Stripe…

I hope...

+

The army officer has left and the social workers are sitting on the sofa, a round black woman and thin white woman beside her, both very smiley, in a grave-faced way. Esme sits in the armchair. I'm alone on the other sofa, the smaller one.

"So, what happens now?" I ask, hugging my knees, my voice very small. "Who will pay Esme?"

The social workers exchange glances with each other, then with Esme, who sits very straight-backed and stiff, watching them.

"Well, Miri," the older social worker speaks quietly, her curly hair bouncing around her head like black wire-wool. "Things are a bit complicated, due to you having no family."

"I have a mother. Apparently."

The social worker winces, then tries to smile, her teeth white against her deep brown skin. "Yes, technically, you have a mother, but she is not...not able to look after you, so—"

"You mean she doesn't want to."

The social worker sighs. "She doesn't want to, no."

"That's why Esme looks after me."

"Yes, we understand that. And we've already evaluated Miss Wilcox thoroughly, so we already know what's what."

"What is what?" I stare at them, hugging my knees tighter.

"The situation with Miss Wilcox." The social worker shifts her position, addressing Esme instead of me. "Miss Wilcox, this is the situation. The criteria for fostering are very strict, and...well, there are reasons why you do not meet those criteria."

Esme's mouth parts slightly in shock. Dismay fills her eyes—and something else I can't make out. She can't foster me? What does that mean? My heart's pounding, faster and faster...

"I...I don't?" Anger fills her eyes. "Is it my dismissal from midwifery? Because that—"

The other social worker jumps in hastily, her straight blond hair swinging as she pushes her glasses up her nose. "Miss Wilcox, we can explain it all in more detail later, and we would be happy to do so."

"Right now," says the older lady, "let me simply go on to say that the criteria for adoption are slightly different, and in light of the fact that you have been the primary nurturer of this child from birth, I'm happy to be able to tell you that you are eligible to adopt him."

Relief explodes inside me. I let out the breath I didn't realize I was holding and smile for the first time since they told me about Dad. Everything will be okay, after all. Esme can simply adopt me.

The social workers are still looking at Esme. "Of course," says the older one, "we don't need an answer on the spot and there would be the usual procedures to follow. Presumably you have been paid up to the end of the month and whatever your decision, you will be happy to remain until that time?"

"I..." Esme looks like someone's just hit her in the face with a dead fish. "I was paid in arrears, actually..."

"Oh...well, I imagine you'll be happy to take a few days to think about it—"

"No," Esme interrupts. "No, I don't need a few days."

My heart swells, warmth soothing the terrible raw gash Dad's death has just hacked through it. I've lost him, but I've still got Esme.

"Of course, I love Miri very much," says Esme. "He's a very special boy. But he's not my son. I've put my life on hold for so long, to take care of him, but adoption is different. There are things I want to do, things I can't possibly do if I'm working flat out to support a child. I can't possibly."

She looks at me at last. I'm staring at her, my mouth open, my mind blank with shock. It feels like she's just pulled out a gun and shot me.

"I'm so sorry, Miri. But I'm sure you understand. Adoption...well, it's different, isn't it?"

And even now, her eyes slide away from the ugly scar on my face.

CHAPTER 7

"Buonasera, Miri. How are you feeling?"

It's Margaret's radiant, ugly face that greets me when I wake up.

"Awful," I whisper. I look like Frankenstein's monster. If Esme didn't want me then, who will ever want me now? I shudder. "I don't want to talk about me. Tell me more about you. Did your father like you better, once he'd won the war and become even more famous?"

Margaret sighs. "I'm afraid not. If anything, he was even more fearful of me being discovered. He felt that the *palazzo's* crypt was not nearly so safe a hiding place for me as my little cell had been, but he feared to return me thence because war might soon break out again."

"What did he do?"

"After the war ended, the talk in Mercatello was all about how miracles were taking place at the tomb of one Fra Giacome, a Franciscan tertiary who had been buried in the not-so-far-distant Cita di Castello. Many people were being healed. At first, my father dismissed the news, thinking it the usual gossip of over-excitable pilgrims. It grieves me to say that my father did not believe that God cared about human beings, thus the idea of divine healings was incredible to him. However, when learned men, doctors and lawyers, also began to report such healings...

"Well, my mother suggested they should take me to the holy friar's tomb in the hope that I might be healed. I realize now the attraction that visiting a new city must also have held for her. But I think she did hope, a little. My father...I would like to think he hoped too, but maybe he always planned...something else."

"What? Were you healed?" I demand, then glance at her. "Oh, clearly not. But what happened? Your father didn't do something to you, did he?" Her father must have been a monster, not to see what a sweet, kind daughter he had.

"Not exactly." She sighs, folding her hands demurely on her knees. "We reached Castello without incident, a long day's journey over hard mountain roads. In the morning, after we spent the night at the best inn in Castello, my father made enquiries around the town. He returned more excited than I could have imagined, completely convinced that real healings were taking place. I think then he truly did hope I would be cured of my deformities and blindness. He even called me 'dear child.' He never had before. Oh, I was so happy, I wept, Miri."

That moment of joyful relief when I thought Esme was about to adopt me fills my mind, choking up my throat. I can't speak, but thankfully Margaret continues unprompted.

"They took me to the church where the tomb lay, and we all received confession and Holy Communion. At least—" she sighs heavily "they led me to believe that they did, though it was not true. Since they showed so little interest in the Sacraments usually—imagine my joy when I thought they had received. Then they left me as close to the tomb of Fra Giacomo as they could get me in the crush and ordered me to pray with all my might for a cure. I obeyed, of course. I prayed ever so hard. That the Lord might cure me or whatever He willed."

"Whatever he willed?" I exclaim. "You were at the site of miraculous cures and you risked it all by adding *that?"*

"Of course," smiled Margaret. "What use would it be to be whole and unblemished if it were not God's will? If it were not something that would benefit me, and others, and draw me closer to Him? *Of course* I asked for whatever He willed. I suppose it was not what my parents intended, but I was too naive to realize that."

She gives a tiny, lady-like shrug of her hunched shoulders. "Well, they waited for some time at a distance, confident that important people like them would be granted a miracle, but nothing happened and they grew bored. Unbeknown to me, to fill in the time, they set off to see the sights in the city. I was not really conscious of the hours passing, I was praying so deeply. I did not notice them return, much later. How could I, with so much noise, and such a crush of persons around me?

"I prayed and prayed all that long day, until the crowd thinned. The bells tolled out the various hours, and still I waited for my parents to come and collect me. My parents' manner had been a little odd for the whole of the journey, but I refused to think on it. But finally my prayer was interrupted by a Franciscan lay brother who had come to close the church for the night, urging everyone to leave. And it was only then that I realized they were no longer in the church."

"What?" I gasp. "Where were they?"

"Many leagues away, riding hard for Mercatello. After they had returned to the church and seen that I had clearly not been cured, they hurried back to the inn, took the horses and their armed escort, and left immediately."

"How could they do that to you?"

"You really need to ask, *caro* Miri?"

My throat swells closed again, pain tearing my

chest in two. No, I don't need to ask. I don't need her to explain a thing.

"But what did you do?" At least I had social workers and foster-carers waiting to take me in charge.

"Well, the lay brother was kind enough to lead me out of the church, since I did not know the way. I assured him that my parents would be back very soon to collect me, so, reluctantly, he left me on the church steps. I was determined to wait there until they came, so as not to alarm or worry them by my absence. I assumed some terrible accident had befallen them, to delay them so grievously."

She smiles the saddest smile yet, but even that is full of peace. "By the time the sun rose, I had accepted that I might never be with them again, that a fatal accident must have occurred. It was only when some kind beggars found me and took me to seek after my parents that the testimony of the innkeeper and gate guards forced me to accept the truth: that my mother and father had mercilessly abandoned me, a twenty-year-old, gently-reared young lady, blind, crippled, and helpless, without a penny to her name, in a strange city."

CHAPTER 8

I don't know what the nurse gave me. No poison, but I'm struggling to wake up properly since Margaret left. I lie in a heavy silence, unable to drag my eye open. The pain seems further away, but when a thought does crawl through my mind, too often it's a glimpse of pins. Pins, pins, more pins. Sticking out of me.

Is it morning? Evening?

Finally, a little gasp from Kara sharpens my attention. Her feet patter quickly across the room—I'm learning to recognize different footsteps, I spend so much time half-awake with my eyes closed.

"Llewey!"

"Kara!" They must be embracing, because his deep, familiar, lilting voice sounds muffled.

"I'm so glad you're here."

"How is he?"

"Oh, Llewey!" Kara drops her voice. "He wanted to

see the pins and everything. And then he was so upset. But Llewey..." Her voice cracks slightly, then goes even softer, "Llewey, I think he still doesn't understand how bad it is. About his eye and everything else. But he's so weak and tired. I haven't had the heart to tell him."

"Oh, Kara..." Llewellyn's deep voice is gentler than usual. I think he's hugging her again. For a second, a fierce yearning stabs me, for him to be hugging *me*, like Dad used to.

"I had to tell him about Stripe. And poor Mr. Evans," Kara whispers. "I think he was very upset. But you know how he is...he doesn't show it much."

"He has to know, Kara. And the rest. Maybe when the doctor comes next, we can all sit down with him and...and talk."

"But they don't know much, yet. It's all so...so up in the air."

"I know. But he'll feel better just to know he's not being kept in the dark. Can you imagine what it must feel like to him, never being in control of anything in his life? We have to tell him."

Kara draws in a deep breath. "Yes. You're right. Now you're here, it will be easier." Her voice goes brisker. "Have they found you a room? Have you eaten? Miri's still asleep; the nurse had to sedate him after... Well, let's grab some food quickly and I'll bring you up to date."

"Okay. Hang on." Heavier footsteps tread across

the floor. Rough fingertips touch my forehead, followed by a kiss. And a deep lilting voice, speaking quick, quiet words. "Keep fighting, Miri. We love you."

Once they're gone, I wonder if I dreamed the last bit. I'm on morphine, after all. Probably I dreamed it. But what did Kara mean, that I don't understand how bad it is? I mean, it looks awful, I saw! But...my eye. Why did she mention my eye?

I hope that doctor turns up soon. I'll need to wake up properly, though. I mustn't overreact again, ever. 'Cause being sedated...really...sucks...

Yep, I'm swimming away again, into blackness...

+

"Why should I?" I snap, when Llewellyn mentions chores. "I'm not your slave. You're getting paid to look after me; you think I don't know that? Do you think I'm stupid?"

Llewellyn listens to my outburst with an impassive face.

"If you want to be just a foster kid then no, you don't need to do chores," he tells me. "But Kara and I have been quite upfront about the fact that in a year or so we hope to be allowed to adopt you. And if you're going to be a member of this family, you'll have to pull your weight. No room for slackers in a farming family. So of course we're hoping you'll want to be part of this family and to start as you mean to go on, but the choice is yours."

He rests a hand on my shoulder for a moment as he moves towards the barn door. "I'll let you think it over. I'll be in the workshop if you want to talk some more."

Once he's gone, I stand staring after him. Heck, he's a clever Welshman, isn't he? Dangling adoption as the ultimate carrot to get free labor from me. I can see right through him. I run a finger over my scar, my dented cheekbone. No one's adopting me. *I'm not that dumb.*

But...I kick irritably against the wooden wall of the old barn. But...

What if it is true? *I can't silence that tiny voice.* What if it's true and you blow it because you're not prepared to feed a few chickens?

It's not true! *I yell at the little voice.* Perfect kids get adopted. Not Scarface!

But.

But.

But.

Does it even matter if it's true? If I blow this, they're putting me in a children's home until I'm eighteen. They've already made that very clear. This is my last chance in a family placement. I'd rather stay here and shovel some manure in a foster family than get stuck in a home, listening to 'Scarface, Scarface, Scarface' all evening and night and morning as well as all day at school.

Argh! What choice have I got?

I march into the workshop. "I'll do the chores," *I announce.* "Of course I want to be part of this family."

Two can play at this game. They want my labor. I want to stay. We can use each other. Fair's fair, right?

+

I'm awake again. And the doctor's come. Llewellyn and Kara are sitting on one side of the bed, and she's sitting on the other.

Kara keeps reaching out to stroke the tuft of hair over my left forehead. I've figured out, after seeing myself, why she isn't stroking my hands. Because they're like pincushions and strapped to boards. I shudder at the memory.

"Are you okay, Miri?"

Quickly, I muster a smile for her. "I'm fine." I don't want to get sedated again. Not now the doctor's here and I'm about to find out stuff. I must stay calm.

The doctor speaks rapidly to Kara and Llewellyn for a few minutes, using a lot of long complicated medical words. They nod a lot and clutch each other's hands. About the time when, despite all my efforts to remain Iceman Miri, I'm about to scream with frustration — or interrupt — she turns her attention to me.

"Miri, I expect you didn't understand a lot of that. I'll try and explain. You know you were unconscious for over two weeks?"

I stare at her, shocked. I shake my head. "Why?"

"You had serious internal injuries. You were too sick to be conscious. I'll be honest with you, we weren't sure if you were going to make it. But you pulled around, and the damaged organs are healing well. So that's good news."

"What's the bad news?"

"Well, there are your other injuries. You have a very great number of broken bones. Not just snapped in half, like a straight-forward broken arm that can be put in plaster, but shattered. You've undergone extensive surgery to get the shattered pieces back in position and initial x-rays are promising. Most of it seems to be knitting together."

"That's...good, right?" Why does she still look so serious?

"Of course. It's very good. But you need to understand, Miri, when bones are shattered to that extent, once they've knitted, they may not be quite the right shape. That matters a lot with joints. And they may not be as strong. You also have a lot of nerves in your limbs, and it's too soon to be sure the extent of the damage to those."

"What are you saying?"

"I'm saying..." She pauses, meeting my eye firmly. "I'm saying, we don't yet know if you will be able to walk again or use your hands and arms reasonably normally."

My jaw drops open. "But..." I splutter, "but...you said it was *knitting*..."

"But the healed bones and joints may be too weak and misshapen to bear your weight. And that's assuming your nerves still work properly. There's always physical therapy, of course, which can help enormously, and they are making some incredible advances in repairing damaged nerves. So, even if, once your bones are healed, you cannot walk immediately, that doesn't mean that it will be permanent. But you need to prepare yourself for being dependent on a wheelchair, or even bed-bound, for quite a while. And possibly forever.

"The very best you can hope for, the very best, is that you might be able to get around by yourself on crutches. But I don't wish to raise your hopes beyond reason. That is the best possible case scenario and it doesn't seem likely at the moment."

I stare at her, swallowing hard, fighting to make sense of this in my mind. My thoughts ricochet around. I can't catch them. Calm. I must stay calm or they'll stick a needle in me and the doctor will go and I won't know everything. I can't think, I can't...

"Is there anything else?" I don't know how I speak so levelly. Kara and Llewellyn shoot me anxious looks.

The doctor moistens her lips. "You'll need plastic surgery in due course, to help with the burn scars on your face and the side of your head, but they're not life-threatening. The scar from where the farm implement tore your cheek can be dealt with at the same time. But, ah, your eye...so far, it's not looking promising."

I close my good eye, fighting for control, fighting not to just start screaming and never stop. Finally, I open it again. "Promising? What does that mean?"

"It's looking likely you'll be almost completely

blind in that eye. It was very badly burned."

I stare around the room, trying to tell how serious this is, compared to everything else. Things do look kind of flat, but I can see fine. I think?

"How much does that matter?"

The doctor looks relieved, as though she was sure this last thing was going to give me the screaming heebie-jeebies. "For daily life, you'll be able to manage fine. But having two eyes gives a person what we call 'depth perception.' It means you can judge how far away things are from you and from each other. You'll be a little clumsier as a result of not having it. And," another breath, and she adds reluctantly, "you may not be able to get a driver's license with only one good eye."

"Never?"

She hesitates. "Experienced drivers who lose an eye can sometimes regain their license after a period of adjustment. But for you, as a learner driver, it could be…difficult."

No driver's license…

"Why are you even showing me this?" I ask Llewellyn, when he sits me down in the tractor and starts pointing out to me the different gear levers and pedals. "I mean, it is interesting, but…"

He grins. "Don't you know you can get your provisional tractor license next year?"

"When I'm fourteen?"

He nods.

"No way!" I yelp. Suddenly I'm sitting forward in the driver's seat, looking around eagerly. "Hey, show me, show me!"

"That I will. We're going to have you baling hay and hauling muck in no time, you wait."

I just grin back. More chores, well, it's a farm. I'm already learning that farm and work go together. But I'm going to get my driver's license! Tractor only, but hey! That's so cool!

...I glance at Llewellyn. He's looking seriously at the doctor, still holding Kara's hand.

No driver's license.

My stomach begins to slide down a long, greasy tunnel into pitch blackness.

Heck, no driver's license, why am I worrying about that? If I can't even walk or use my hands...I won't be able to do any chores at all, even the non-driving ones.

No chores. I can't pull my weight in a farming family. Not one bit.

Not ever again.

No room for slackers in a farming family.

So that means...

...that means they can't possibly adopt me.

I don't think anyone has stuck a needle in me. But everything seems to be...seems to be fading into blackness...again...

CHAPTER 9

I dream about Margaret.

She's defending her absent parents' actions to a crowd of outraged beggars, so fiercely, announcing that after all, she is a grown woman and it is quite time for her to earn her own keep. Soon she's begging on church steps and washing in public fountains. Sleeping in doorways, dodging the city watch. Sweetly thanking the tradesmen who allow her to overnight in their stable or pigsty in the dead of winter, thus preserving her life through to another dawn. She rejoices in imitating the Lord, who 'had nowhere to lay his head,' whether through sleeping in a stall as He did as an infant or in being spat upon by a passerby. She doesn't understand why people pity her.

I dream of how her joy in life, her unshakeable conviction of God's love, her ability to see the good in every situation, all gradually infect the other beggars, changing their lives inwardly so that an existence that once seemed only barely preferable to death becomes specked with blessings.

I see respectable townsfolk stopping to chat with her, drawn by her unfailing cheerfulness and patience. Marveling at her joy. Arguing with one another about whether she is a sweet, genuine young woman or a beggar putting on a very astute act. As the months pass, the town grows more and more interested—and deeply divided. Is 'little Margaret' a fraud, they whisper, or a saintly unfortunate?

The dream stays in my mind as I wake. Was that how it was for my new friend? Did she simply find her feet as a beggar and stay happy? Something about Margaret seems oddly familiar, now that my head is a little clearer. What is it? She did say we'd sort of met. When? I wish she'd visit me again.

When I come *really* properly awake, or as awake as I seem to be able to manage at the moment, Margaret drops out of my mind. The doctor's words consume me. Bedbound for the rest of my *life?* The best I can possibly hope for—and not likely, mind—being on *crutches?* I can't do farm work on crutches. I'll never even be able to ride again.

The cleaner was right. I'd be better off dead. I'm going to be alone and unwanted for the rest of my life. A hideous monster, unlovable, rotting away in care. Why did they save me? I wish they would come and give me that injection, finish the abortion, make my mother happy. There's no reason for me to be alive, none...

I keep my eye closed until I can't bear the boredom any more. Then I stare up at the square ceiling tiles, ignoring everyone, until that's too boring. I close my eye again. Kara and Llewellyn hover, speaking. Doctors and nurses hover. I refuse to respond. I refuse to eat. I refuse to drink. Maybe if I ignore everything long enough, what's left of my body will just...stop. I want so much to stop. For everything to go away, forever.

Kara's speaking to me again. I keep my eye closed.

Go away. You can't adopt me now. Sooner or later, you're going to give me back. And they're going to put me in some care home. And that's going to be my life. Unloved, forever. Don't try to make me hope. I'm not that stupid. Just leave me alone...

+

When I walk up the lane and into the Williams's farmyard, the first Friday of my homeschooling career, I hear the thud of hooves from behind the barn. I'm slightly early, so I walk around to see what's going on.

There's a large rectangular area of sand back there, fenced off from the field, and Catherine and John are riding horses around it. I watch, fascinated, as somehow they get the big animals to do just what they want. Catherine makes her horse do a pirouette on the spot — I can't tell how. John's horse does a neat, slow-motion sort of gallop. Or maybe a 'canter,' that's what the stranger standing in the sandy field calls it. Then the stranger puts up some jumps and...wheee...over they go, flying on their horses' backs.

I know about horse-riding, of course. But I've never seen it in the flesh. Just odd snatches on TV. It looks amazing. I can't stop imagining what it must feel like to fly over a jump like that, the horse's muscles bunching beneath you. To be so much one with a horse that you can make it dance around like that without any sign you're telling it to do anything. My mind teems with imaginings.

Before long, the stranger glances at her watch. "Okay, Catherine, that will do. I want ten minutes with John to work on this little problem of Whisky getting on the wrong foot all the time."

"Okay, thanks," says Catherine. "See you next week."

The stranger holds the gate open and Catherine rides through it. When she slides off and takes the reins to lead the horse, she notices me and smiles. She's always been nice to me, so far.

"Oh, hi, Miri. We should've told you, we have our riding lesson on Friday because it's way cheaper not to have it at the weekend. So we start school a few minutes later today."

I can't stop looking at the horse, at the leather straps on its head, at the...the what's it...saddle, on its back. It looks so tall and strong and alive. Majestic.

Catherine glances from me to it. "Oh, uh, do you want a quick ride, Miri?"

A ride? Do I want one? I don't think I've ever wanted

anything so much—except people to love me.

But I'm not that dumb. If I say yes, let her know how much I'd like it, she'll laugh and say something mean about how she was only joking, my face might scare her horse.

"No," I say shortly.

She looks surprised. "Oh. Um, well, d'you want to help me take his tack off and rub him down?"

Hmm. That sounds like work. A chore. I guess she might let me help with that.

"Okay."

As we walk off, she actually places the leather straps—the reins—in my hand. "Here, you can lead him. I don't think he'll give you trouble, he's tired enough. Hold the reins a little tighter—not too tight—just so you can almost feel his mouth. That's right."

I can't believe I'm walking along leading a horse. A real live horse. He's beautiful, with his glossy coat and big eyes. Oh, I would love to ride him!

"He's a bit of a handful for a beginner, when he's fresh," Catherine is saying. "But once he's had some exercise, he's not too frisky. Maybe next week you'll feel like riding. If you do, come a little early since John may have some one-to-one again. And Mum won't mind if we start school half an hour later, if it's so you can have a proper ride while Polo's in the right mood."

I keep shooting looks at her, the whole time she's showing me how to take the 'tack' off and rub Polo all over with a brush—"no, much harder, Miri, you have to give it some wellie; yes, that's it"—trying to judge if she's sincere. Maybe she's just trying to get me up here early next Friday so she can laugh at me. But she's letting me touch her horse; she let me lead him.

"Pony, Miri," she corrects me before long. "When I outgrow dear Polo, it'll be a horse for me. But Polo is a pony. Not a polo pony, though."

It takes her until we reach the farmhouse to explain about polo, the horseback game, as opposed to Polo, the crunchy mints, which is what her horse...sorry, pony...is named after and likes to eat, for a special treat only because they're bad for his teeth.

I watch her all week, trying to catch her being nasty to me. Does she really mean it?

I call myself a fool, but I can't help it. When Friday comes around again, I hurry up to the Williams's farm bright and early. I even wear sensible shoes.

And I get my first ride, ever.

+

Kara and Llewellyn are talking softly. To each other, not to me. They think I'm asleep. My plan isn't working. After I refused three meals, the medical staff simply put the feeding tube back down my nose and into my stomach. Now they can feed me what they like. I'm still refusing to speak to anyone, though. Especially Kara and Llewellyn. They will give me back. I know they will.

No room for slackers in a farming family.

"I thought we were doing the right thing." Llewellyn sounds anguished. "I thought he'd feel better, to know. Now I'm not so sure."

"No, you *were* right, Llewey. We couldn't keep it a secret. He just—" Kara's voice shakes "—he just needs... a bit more time. It must've been such a shock."

"I can't bear to see him like this. I feel like it's my fault—" Shockingly Llewellyn's voice breaks. I hear Kara soothing him.

Llewellyn was supposed to have gone home after the weekend, but he hasn't. That's my fault. The sound of him sobbing makes me feel... But I keep my eyes closed tighter than ever, trying to wrap my heart in protection, more and more of it, like wrapping a bale of silage in layer upon layer of thick black plastic, the way Mr. E showed me only a few weeks ago.

I will not allow myself to hope. I will not allow myself to care. I'm a worthless, scarred thing, and no one will ever want me now. That is the truth, and there is no beauty or love. Not for me.

CHAPTER 10

"Oh my word, there's a miracle in this room, right now!"

A loud, cheerful voice snaps my eye open and draws my gaze before I can control myself. A priest stands by the bed. I know he's a priest because he's wearing a long black dress with a wide sash and lots of buttons up the front, though he seems totally unselfconscious about it. His skin's so dark he'd look black from top to bottom if he wasn't smiling so wide, his teeth like two rows of little pearls glinting at me. Pearls...

Yeah, I'd *much* rather it was Margaret standing by the bed. But I haven't seen her for days. I hope she's okay. I never did ask why she was at the hospital. I assumed she'd come to visit the sick, but maybe she's ill.

"Oh, that's really *hilarious*, you know," I snap at the

unwelcome visitor. "You *really* think I haven't heard them all by now? I'm thirteen, not three!"

He grins even more widely, plunking himself down in the chair, which creaks slightly. He's young and fit-looking, and as sports teachers love to point out, muscle is heavier than fat.

"What are you so happy about?" I demand.

"Wel-l-l, now." He smiles, eyes glinting. "I made a bet with your folks that I couldn't get you to speak to me—and I just won it, didn't I?"

I stare at him. Seriously? Talk about bare-faced cheek! Here I am, lying here so sick, and he's *betting* about—

"Un-be-lievable," I say, in that dignified, disgusted voice that social workers use when they hear that I've got into a particularly bad fight.

It has no effect on him whatsoever. He just smiles, a bit more gently. "Well, they were feeling so down. I was trying to cheer them up."

Kara and Llewellyn made that bet? Curiosity gets the better of me. "What do you win?"

"A rosary said for my chosen intention. Today, that's you. So they won't be doing anything they weren't going to do anyway, will they? A very harmless bet."

"Well, you can go away. I don't want to talk to anyone."

"That's a shame. Since conversation is something

you can enjoy as well as ever."

Huh? I can't help thinking about that for a moment. He's right. The realization does nothing to sweeten my mood.

"That's all I *can* do, didn't they tell you? Lie here like Frankenstein's monster and talk. And rot. Nothing else. Ever, probably. So go away and leave me alone."

"That doesn't make sense, you know. If I was asking you to jump up and play football with me, it would."

"Shove off."

"Sorry, I've been hard at work visiting the wards and I need to sit here and rest for a few minutes."

I glare at him. Liar! He looks lively as a flea. I want his cheerfulness out of my presence. It grates against me like a cheese grater stripping my skin. How dare he smile like that? How dare he joke? Heck, if I could move my hands I would *throw* something at him, make him leave.

Except I'm not sure it would. Which is even more annoying than not being able to do it.

"Am I making you angry, Miri? Good."

"What? Why is that good?"

"Because you're feeling something towards someone other than yourself. Not a very positive emotion, it's true. But better than nothing."

"I hate you!"

"That's impressive, seeing that you don't even

know me. My name is Father Thomas, by the way."

"I don't care what your name is. Go away."

"Why? What were you doing that I interrupted?"

"Doing? What the heck could I be doing?"

"Well, you act like I'm interrupting something important. What?"

I stare at him, my throat tight. I can't hold the words back. "I'm lying here trying to wish myself to death, okay? What do you think I'm doing?"

His gaze is so serious, now, I almost want the cheerfulness back. "Yeah, I figured," he says softly.

"Look, will you please go away?" I beg. "My life isn't going to fix itself because some priest who fancies himself a comedian comes and grins at me."

He just smiles sadly. "It's going to take more than a grin and a few jokes, isn't it? Fair enough. Have you tried asking for help?"

"From you? What can you do?"

"From Someone rather more powerful than me. From my Boss."

The rage that overwhelms me is like nothing I've ever felt before. It burns through every inch of me, every cell, every hair. If I could spit at him I would, but with that feeding tube still running down my nose I don't get a drink very often and my mouth is too dry to muster saliva.

"Don't you *dare* talk to me about your boss! He *hates* me, do you understand? He hates me more than anyone on this planet! More than my mum. More than— He *hates* me! If you try to tell me He loves me...if you *dare* tell me He loves me!" I'm spluttering, inarticulate with rage. "He...He almost gave me everything I ever wanted and then He just...He took it away. He just... Don't you say it, I'll...I'll get off this bed and...I *will*..."

I try to move but pain explodes from a hundred places and I lie very still, gasping, glaring, probably foaming at the mouth for all I know, but with the morphine I can't tell. I don't care. If he put his hand near my teeth I would *bite* it. I would bite it *off*.

He's on his feet, leaning over me.

"Miri, please calm down. I won't say anything more, I promise. I'll leave. Please, calm down..."

I hurt too much to speak. I just glare and pant.

"Miri, may I pray for you before I leave?" He speaks very softly—nervously.

I feel a stab of involuntary admiration for his persistence, though I want to bite his prayers in half, savage them, shake them like a dog shaking a rat. I don't even know why I stay silent. But I do.

He takes my silence for permission. I expect him to speak the words I've just forbidden him to utter, so I brace myself for another stomach-wringing surge of anger and hate—but he just lays his hand very lightly on my head—the left side, of course—bows his head, and murmurs under his breath for a while. Even though I don't know what he's saying—or maybe because—it's oddly soothing.

"Amen," he says, finally, then meets my eye firmly. "A *lot* of people care what happens to you, Miri," he says, "*including God.*"

After coming so close to the forbidden words, he makes a very hasty retreat. But I just stare after him, swamped in confusion.

If God hates me, why did He send that annoying priest to visit me? What would Margaret think if she'd heard my outburst? But how *can* God love me? But *she* loves God, despite everything He did...*did* He do it to her? What did she say about the evil one taking advantage of everything...even random chance...trying to separate us from God...?

Heck, I hurt. I hurt so much. Every bit of me, body and soul. I can't think about it now.

The pain eases a little as I go on lying still, but not much. I was an idiot to so much as try to twitch. When Kara returns, I ask her to fetch a nurse to increase my morphine. I wish they would raise it all the way, put me right to sleep.

A lot of people care what happens to you, Miri.

Yeah, Kara wouldn't let that happen. But that's not fair, not when she's going to give me back, sooner or later. Not fair at all...

CHAPTER 11

"Ah, *caro* Miri, you look so sad."

Margaret has just eased her twisted little body up into the bedside chair, looking tinier than ever after Father Thomas just sat there.

"Where have you been?" I peer at her. "Are you okay? I missed you."

"Oh, I am very well, Miri. And I have not been far away, I promise."

Although I'm glad to see her, I'm very afraid that if she asks me about myself, we'll get onto the subject of Father Thomas's visit—or rather, what I said during it. I don't want her disappointed with me.

"Did you spend the rest of your life as a beggar in Castello?" I ask quickly.

"Why, no. I spent only a couple of years with my dear 'family of the streets.' Then—it was a beautiful thing—the poor of the city more or less adopted me.

None of them could afford to have me live with them long-term. So they moved me from house to house, to spread out the burden."

"The poor?" My image of the poor in the old days is of people living all in one room, along with the livestock, without enough to eat. "That was generous of them."

"Wasn't it? But God blessed them for it. You would not believe how many families stopped arguing or returned to the Faith or were reconciled in diverse ways after taking me in."

I can't help smiling slightly, to hear her credit God for this. Surely it was her sweet and generous nature and good example?

Oblivious, she goes on, "Many even experienced quite unexpected improvements to their material situation. It became quite a widely-known phenomenon."

Material improvements? Like, more money and better jobs and health? Hmm. Maybe God did have something to do with it.

"Did you ever find a permanent home?"

"Oh yes. But not until quite a long time later. The poor opened their homes to me for a year or two. For a while I even ran an informal little school to teach their children, as a way to return their kindness. But the sisters of the local convent, the Monastero di Santa Margherita — forgive me if I do not name their order — came to hear about me. They felt that a girl of my background should not be forced to live so rootless an existence and that it would be more appropriate for me to enter their community."

"Really? That must have suited you down to the ground!"

She smiles. "Ah, it was not quite that simple. First of all, there were three requirements at the time to enter a religious order. Irreproachable character, legitimate birth, and freedom from serious physical handicaps. They were satisfied as to the first, but since I was not prepared to expose my parents by naming them, they had no way to be assured of the second. And the third was obviously a serious obstacle."

"So you couldn't join them?" Typical. My heart sinks. Just when I thought she might've found a home, after all.

"They decided to leave the decision in the hands of the local bishop. He made inquiries into my baptism in Mercatello, and I believe he must have received copies of my baptismal certificate and my parents' marriage certificate, which means he must have discovered the state's greatest living war hero's shocking secret. But, I am glad to say, he did not reveal their identities.

"Hardly surprising." She sighs. "Not long before, a great lord not so unlike my father had even kidnapped the Pope himself and held him captive. He treated him so badly that the poor man died not long after he was released. So the bishop simply confirmed to the nuns that I was legitimate without telling them anything more. And he waived the third, problematic, requirement."

"So you did join the convent! That's great!" I'm surprised how happy I am for her, how deeply I've allowed myself to feel for her. Why am I being so unguarded? Don't I know better? But somehow I know that Margaret is different. That she isn't going to hurt me. I don't know how, but I do.

"Oh, I entered the convent. It was the happiest day of my life, Miri. I cannot tell you how happy. No longer did I have to impose on the poor, taking resources from their own families. And finally, I could live in quiet again, quiet for prayer and reflection, quiet to help me live in as great a union with Our Lord as possible. Such joy!"

"I bet the nuns loved you."

"They made me most welcome. Indeed, they were pleasantly surprised that I could do all manner of little jobs and chores and make myself very useful—I fear they had not expected me to be able to do anything practical for others. I made my promise to follow the Rule of the Order, and everything seemed perfect. Finally, I was a valued member of a community and had the love and affection I'd craved for so long. To say nothing of the security I'd lost when I arrived in Castello."

Love and security...my heart swells with a mixture

of gladness for her and something like envy...then sinks. "Seemed?"

"Ah, you are very sharp, Miri. Yes, all went well for about a year. So well, that I'll be honest with you, I began to worry. I felt...how can I explain? I had come to the convent to labor for the good of souls, in prayer and penance. And there I was, so happy, enjoying the life so much. I began to fear that my sinfulness had led me to be judged unworthy to suffer any more on Our Lord's behalf. It was the only thing that marred my happiness."

"That you *weren't* suffering?" Disbelief fills my voice. "But you'd had a lifetime's suffering already! Why shouldn't you be happy?"

"Because as a very young child I had offered my will to my Lord, offered to follow Him along the road to Calvary, to the bitter end. Suffering was the mold that shaped my holiness and the most powerful help I could offer up for others."

I frown. Her conviction that suffering is so helpful and so potent is something I'm still struggling to understand. *I* just wish my sufferings would go away.

"Well, I needn't have worried," she goes on, when I remain silent. "The other sisters began to notice that my 'initial enthusiasm' as they tended to call it, was taking an extraordinarily long time to wear off. Religious communities, you see, are founded by truly saintly individuals who write challenging Rules which communities initially have the zeal to fulfill in both letter and spirit. But as the generations pass, almost inevitably the strict interpretation of the Rule is gradually eroded. It was centuries since our Rule was written and discipline was seriously lacking in my convent."

"Did you reform them, then?" I ask, confident that the answer will be yes.

Margaret smiles sadly. "I did try. So much was wrong. The periods of silence went unobserved. Visitors came and went to the parlor constantly. Sisters thought nothing of accepting expensive gifts. It hurt me to see it, Miri. All of it explained away with would-be convincing sounding arguments about charity and us living in more enlightened times and there being no harm in it.

"But I could not forget that I had promised, promised *God*, to follow the Rule. Not to follow some watered-down interpretation of it. The Rule. As written. What else could I do but follow it? I discussed it, over and over, with my confessor, and he supported my decision. But the other sisters hated it."

"Why? I mean, they could just carry on doing their own thing, right?"

"They could and did. But every time they saw me doing what, deep down, they knew they should have been doing too, it disturbed their conscience and thus their comfort. Eventually, the Prioress ordered me straight-out to give up my 'excesses.' Such a crisis I never underwent before or after, Miri. Do you know how important obedience is for a religious? How was I to choose between an order from my superior, whom I was bound to obey as I would Christ, and the Rule which I had promised Christ Himself I would obey? I sought the advice of my confessor yet again."

"And he said continue as you were?"

She nods. "Yes, Miri. So I did. Disobedience to a superior being such a grave fault, I was put out of the convent forthwith, with no more than my crutch and the clothes on my back."

"No way!"

"Yes. For the second time, my whole life lay in ruins around me and this time it was almost too much. The evil one launched a supreme attack upon me. I felt as though all I had ever received for trying to serve God faithfully was pain and suffering. Fourteen years of imprisonment, abandonment, living as a beggar, and now this. Clearly I was a fool not to serve God in moderation only, as so many did. If I had only compromised, I would not have been in this desperate situation for a second time."

She bows her head. "It was clear to me that God no longer wanted me or cared about my efforts. I had tried so hard on His behalf, and now I was homeless again. It felt like His back was turned to me. My whole life, no one had wanted me, and now God didn't want me either."

My throat closes up, so tight. I fight to breathe. If

she so much as looks towards me kindly, I'm going to break down and weep. I'm going to *howl*. For a second time, *my* life is in ruins. And God has certainly turned His back on me!

But when she raises her head, her face is calm again, the anguish wiped away. "But then, just when the evil one had almost succeeded in chaining me in the very depths of despair, I remembered."

"What?" I whisper, my voice thin and choked.

"That when Our Lord had hung on the cross for those three agonizing hours, His body broken, the weight of every sin every person who had ever lived or ever would live crushing His soul, He too had reached such a depth of mental and spiritual anguish that He felt Himself abandoned by all, even by His Almighty Father. And He cried out in desolation."

"O God, O God, why have you forsaken me?" I whisper. For a moment, I'm back in a crowded church, sitting beside Dad... No, I'm sitting beside Llewellyn, only weeks ago... Either way, it's Good Friday and Jesus is dying, alone and abandoned...

"But do you know how the psalm ends?" asks Margaret.

"Tell me."

"Posterity shall serve Him; men shall tell of the Lord to the coming generation, and proclaim His deliverance to a people yet unborn, that He has wrought it."

In other words: God wins in the end.

"And you see," Margaret goes on, "Our Lord could not have spoken those words without remembering the rest of the psalm and the triumph of God. Nor was He alone. The holy women and His dearest friend were with Him. Was I, who had promised to dwell always there with them, at the foot of His cross, going to turn away? To abandon Him?

"Never!" She slaps her hand emphatically against the handle of her crutch. "I could not. I picked up my crutch and I wiped my eyes and hobbled on my way, happy to be a beggar again, if that was how the Lord wished me to keep Him company."

CHAPTER 12

The next day, I can't get Margaret's harrowing story out of my mind. In a way, she was more alone than I am. I have Kara and Llewellyn here with me and Margaret too—like Jesus, I'm not *actually* alone, however I feel. She was thrown out on the street with nobody.

But then again...I've only got Kara and Llewellyn for a while longer. They don't want to abandon me when things are so very bad, clearly, but once I'm a bit better...they'll have to give me back. Get a replacement. A whole, undamaged lad to foster and maybe even adopt. A boy who can still do chores and drive a tractor. And get out of bed. And not need every last thing done for him.

So it's only Margaret that counts, really. And she disappears half the time.

Still, I can't help wondering if I was suffering an onslaught of the evil one yesterday, as she would put it.

The anger and hate I felt towards the priest—towards God—were terrifying. A whisper in my mind says I'm quite justified in feeling that way, but I think Margaret would say that was the devil's voice. It can't be a good idea to listen to *him*. No way does he have my best interests at heart. I'm not sure if God does, but no one even *pretends* that the red horned guy does.

I do speak to Kara and Llewellyn, though, for the first time in days. Just to answer them when they say anything to me. I won't let them draw me into conversation, though. I've got to get them out of my heart again, as much as I can, before it happens. So it doesn't hurt too much.

When they go off to the cafeteria to have lunch—they always go together now, as though they need each other's support—I think I'm going to get some time to myself, but only a few minutes later Father Thomas looks in at the doorway.

"Ah, Miri. Good afternoon."

I heave a big, exaggerated sigh, then regret it. The nurse turned my morphine down again this morning, worse luck. "What do *you* want?"

He steps into the room, and a boy follows him in. "I've brought you some company. Daniel's just been having his chemo and I'm giving him a lift home today. But I have a few more visits to make first. So I thought you two could hang out together for a bit."

Chemo? Heck, this priest is unbelievable. Putting

some poor dying boy in here with me and my rage is like shoving a canary into a cat carrier!

"That's just low, Father!" I snap.

He wiggles his fingers in a gesture that might mean either 'behave' or 'have fun,' steps back out and closes the door behind him.

I turn my good eye to Daniel, trying not to glare. I mean, it's not his fault the priest hits below the belt.

Daniel's clearly several years older than me, taller than I realized at first—everyone looks high up, from my bed—all stretched out, like he's grown a lot recently. But extremely thin, and bald, too. That must be from his illness, or maybe the chemo. He sinks into the chair by the bed the way an old person would, as though he's desperately glad to be off his feet. His jeans and top are unremarkable, but he wears a rugged-style crucifix on a leather cord around his neck. His skin is even paler than mine, though whether that's his illness or his natural coloration I can't tell.

And soft grey eyes, watching me so calmly and reminding me slightly of...Margaret. Uh-oh, maybe Father Thomas actually just tossed a cat into a mouse cage!

"Hi," says Daniel. "You're Miracle, right? Cool name."

"I prefer Miri." And because I can't think of anything to say, I blurt, "How old are you, anyway?"

"Sixteen," he says. "Father Thomas said you're

thirteen?"

"Well, I'm fourteen soon, but yeah, he was right about *that*."

"I find Father Thomas is right about lots of things."

"Really." I'm not taking *that* bait! "So, *I* got hit by a runaway tractor and now I'm Frankenstein's monster only less useful. What's wrong with *you?*"

His brow wrinkles slightly at my words, but he just says. "I have leukemia."

"That stinks."

He shrugs. "I've had it since I just turned fifteen. They thought they'd seen it off, but late last year it came back again. It took two rounds of chemo to get rid of it last time, and now I'm on my second round again."

"Is it working?"

He hesitates. "They think so."

Not dying after all, then? The priest didn't choose very well. But... "You don't sound very sure about it."

He shrugs again. "I'm not a doctor. If they say it's working, it probably is."

"So?"

He's silent for a long time. "Well...I don't usually tell people this, but I suppose you don't know me so it won't bother you the same way. So, yeah, it does looks like they may be going to fight it off again, this time. But I have this...it's hard to describe it, so let's just say... inner certainty...that..." he draws an extra breath and says, "that I won't be going to university."

His matter-of-fact words make the hairs on the back of my neck prickle. "Lots of people don't." I try for a light-hearted tone.

His lips turn up in a slight smile. "Yeah, Razim wants to become an apprentice electrician—no university for him. But you know what I mean. My friends talk about the future all the time, now. Katie can't decide between being a nurse or a social worker. And they ask me what I'm going to be, and I just want to say, 'I'm going to be the two of you's prayer support.' But I don't have the heart. Even when I try to tell Father Thomas, he just gets very earnest about how careful we have to be trusting to feelings and private revelations that can't be adequately cross-checked against the Bible or Church teaching. I think he hates the thought that I might...give up. Though he's right, of course—I *could* be wrong. But knowing that doesn't change...y'know."

Doesn't change his 'inner certainty.'

"That's grim," I say.

He cocks his head slightly, as though considering my words. "I don't think so," he says at last. "It reminds me...that I can't take time for granted. It keeps me focused on what's important."

"The pearl in the field." I speak without thinking.

He smiles, with his mouth and with his eyes, too. For a moment, Margaret's radiance shines from his face. "Exactly!"

Yep, no question Daniel is a Jesus-freak. Then again,

my best friend in the whole world is too and I don't mind her. I wish she would come to see me more often.

+

Margaret doesn't visit again, though. Daniel does. Father Thomas brings him around several days that week, at about the same time. When it becomes clear he doesn't intend to ram Jesus down my throat, I don't mind his visits so much. He seems kind—not as kind as Margaret, but who is?—and he does genuinely seem to care, though why, I don't know, when I'm just some much younger foster kid and he's a well-cared for boy from some perfect family. But apparently Father Thomas had to have a huge argument with the doctors—and Daniel with his parents—to get them to let us visit together. Something to do with the fact that if either of us catches something from the other, we might fall off our perch.

"So why are you here, if it's so dangerous for you?" I demand.

Daniel shrugs. "I'd rather come and chat to you than sit alone in some disinfected room hoarding my life like a miser. There are plenty of people I *do* see. It's silly to get so stressy about one more. Anyway, the last time I had a serious infection I ended up in hospital on an antibiotics drip, totally spaced out. And Blessed Carlo Acutis and Blessed Pier Giorgio Frassati came and chilled out by my bed and we had the most amazing conversation. Some of the questions I asked—well, I just wish I'd been able to remember all their answers when I woke up properly. But I remembered enough to know it was awesome!" His eyes shine with the memory.

But...he thinks their answers would have been *true*? I eye him as closely as I can with my one working eye. "Uh...are you saying you thought it was...real?"

He laughs. "Well, obviously not real in the sense that I could have reached out and touched them, physically. They're both dead and in heaven with God. But the Communion of Saints—that's all the people in heaven—they're actually just a hairsbreadth away from us all the time, did you know that? So, I have this theory that when our rational barriers are down—y'know, the parts of our mind that have been stuffed full of the idea that you can't see or talk to dead people—it's that much easier for the Holy Spirit to make us see and interact with a saint. In our head, you know? So, if we're asleep or feverish or on certain drugs, that's when we might be open to an encounter."

"Close encounters of the heavenly kind?" I say in a spooky voice, and we both laugh.

"Kinda."

"Cool theory. What does Father Thomas think?"

"He said, 'Maybe so, Daniel, maybe so. Very plausible.' Endorsement enough!"

"I was supposed to be choosing a saint, actually. When I had my—" But my words choke off in my throat.

"Miri? Are you okay?"

My mind's spinning. My book. Catherine gave me a book. A book about...Saint Margaret of Castello. A nobleman's daughter, born crippled, blind, and a dwarf, in medieval Italy. Imprisoned and later abandoned by her uncaring parents...

How could I have forgotten? Shock…and morphine. So much morphine…

I'm breathing too fast, struggling to get enough air. Margaret? Margaret's a *saint*? Or...Margaret's not real?

What...? How...?

"Miri, talk to me, are you okay? Shall I call the nurses?"

I shake my head. "No!"

"What's wrong?"

"Margaret! My friend... She's...I *thought* she was. But...but I've just realized...she might not even be real!" So much for Margaret not hurting me. My throat feels horribly tight, like I want to cry. Which Miracle Taylor does not do, ever.

"Tell me about it, Miri?" Which is a nice way of saying he's not sure what I'm going on about.

So I tell him. I tell him about her visits and the conversations we've had. How lovely and kind she is, how I felt like she really, really cared. Like she was my best friend, ever.

"So...what do you think?" I ask at last, my voice shaking slightly.

His eyes are wide. "Sounds like you've got yourself a *very* good friend. Wow, I may just have to go to confession for envy. But, uh, I suppose you may not see so much of her, now they're not pumping you quite so full of morphine all the time. That's one of the drugs that lowers the barriers big time, you know."

The pain in my chest eases a bit, at the thought that Margaret might actually be real, even if not *physical*. But how can I know?

"Well, find out more about her, keep talking to her," suggests Daniel, when I voice this question out loud. "I think it will become clearer. Just don't assume you'll *see* her anymore."

CHAPTER 13

"Llewellyn?" He went back to the farm for part of the week, once I was eating and talking again, but it's the weekend and he's back. I'm trying not to be glad to see him, but it's hard.

He looks up from his newspaper and the strained eagerness on his face is painful. "Yes, Miri?"

"I was just wondering...I had a book with me when...when the accident happened. What happened to it?"

He looks a bit anxious, but replies at once. "It was lying beside you, didn't even get burned. We have it here—well, back in the guest accommodation. But...we weren't sure if you'd want to see it or not."

"Yes, I would."

He jumps up, dropping the newspaper. "I can fetch it. Right away. I'll fetch it..."

He's gone before I can even reply.

Since everyone is kind enough to take turns reading the book to me, I gradually learn the rest of Margaret's life story. She still hasn't visited me again. What did she say last time, that she hadn't been 'far away'? That's comforting, even if I can't see her.

Llewellyn reads about how, after being thrown out of the convent, she was subjected to public mockery. Most of those who did not know her well assumed her apparent 'failure' as a nun was proof that she was not a saint after all. Children mobbed her and called her names in the street. Grown-ups made nasty comments in her hearing.

Poor Margaret. Every time she must've thought she could not suffer any more, things got worse for her.

But, gradually, the tide shifted. Margaret claimed so humbly that she was simply not good enough to be a nun, while the nuns, who were supposed to be nice to everyone, said harsh things about her. And slowly, people began to notice the contrast in the behavior and attitudes of the two parties. Not long after that, the shrewdest began to surmise the true reason for her dismissal from the convent. And gradually, the town's opinion of Margaret began to rise again.

"At least she wasn't actually homeless again," says Kara. "The townspeople took her into their homes—and no longer the very poorest of them."

Kara reads the next part—how Margaret, while

going to daily Mass at her favorite church, the Chiesa della Carita, met a group of women called *Mantellate*. They were lay members of the Order of Penance of Saint Dominic. They were women who wanted to live a life more devoted to God but for whatever reason weren't able to enter a convent, so as *Mantellate* they continued to live at home, but under a special rule of life, and always wearing the Dominican religious habit, wherever they went.

"They're the forerunners of the Lay Dominicans," says Daniel, when I tell him. "Only I don't think Lay Dominicans still wear the habit. They wear normal clothes. Except I think they're allowed to wear it when they're dead."

"Huh?"

"You know, in their coffin. To be buried in."

"Oh." Trust Daniel to know that detail.

"Look. This is for you." Daniel holds out a little card, positioning it so I can see it. I'm still not allowed to move my hands. "See, look what she's wearing."

It's a prayer card, with a picture of Saint Margaret on it! They haven't got her face quite right, but she's all little and bent over and ugly, with a crutch under her arm. And she's wearing a nun-like outfit—a white tunic, a leather belt, a long white oblong veil over her head, and a cool-looking black cloak.

"The cloak is called a *mantella*," says Daniel, who's clearly been reading up. "That's why they were called *mantellate.*"

"Honestly," I pretend to be annoyed. "Haven't you heard of spoilers? The Dominican prior and the *mantellate* were still arguing over whether Margaret could even join when Kara went off to lunch, and you go and show me this!"

"Sorry." Daniel grins. "Well, let me put you out of your suspense. They argued for ages, because at the time, *mantellate* were supposed to be older widows, or just once in a blue moon an old married woman could join with her husband's permission. But young women were not permitted to join. But eventually they decided that since Margaret wasn't some frivolous young butterfly, but very mature and sensible, an exception could be made. She was the first young unmarried woman ever recorded to have joined the Order of Penance of Saint Dominic, you know.

"No," he corrects himself, "only the first after the order became more formally recognized in the Church. There was a Blessed Jane—or Giovanna—" he manages a somewhat convincing Italian accent "of Orvieto some years before, but she was basically seen as a one-off. Margaret joining after the lay part of the order had become more official made her a real trailblazer. She paved the way for young unmarried Lay Dominicans like Saint Catherine of Sienna, Saint Rose of Lima, and Blessed Pier Giorgio Frassati."

I feel a stab of pride, as though Margaret really was

my very real friend. I hope she is.

"She carried on staying with different people. Even the rich wanted to have her in their home by then, despite her deformities. She must've been an education to everyone. Where do you want me to put this?"

Daniel waves the card at me.

"Oh, can you stand it up on there...so I can see it? Thanks."

I peer at it once he's put it in position. Yep, I can get a good look at it. I can move my head around properly, now. The burns on my head and down the side of my neck have healed up a lot. I can even poke the call button with my chin, if Kara makes sure to leave it in just the right position. It's hard to believe how wonderful it is, just to be able to *push a button by myself!*

I'm really enjoying Daniel's visits, too. They took the dressings off my face the other day and Kara still refuses to let me look in a mirror. Says it's too soon and there's no point. Daniel doesn't react at all, though. He still simply looks me in the eye and sometimes, for a moment or two I actually forget that I'm Frankenstein's monster and feel like I'm just a boy hanging with a mate. It's a blissful feeling.

Of course, the next moment I remember I can't move and might never be able to walk and it's only a matter of time before Kara and Llewellyn put me back into care. But it's nice while it lasts.

Hmm.

"Daniel?"

He raises his head, blinking slightly. He does nod off, sometimes. "At the beginning of chemo I'm exhausted from the cancer; at the end, I'm exhausted from the chemo," he told me the other day.

"Miri?"

"There's a mirror in the bedside cabinet. Could you get it?"

Daniel tenses. "Um." Silence for a moment. I marshal arguments and pleas, but then he says, "Are you really sure? It's going to look so different once they've done the plastic surgery."

"It won't look as different as they'd like you to think. Less red, mostly. Take a look at my other cheek. That's basic-level National Health Service scar repair for you. Please get the mirror."

Daniel sighs, but he leans his long body forwards and retrieves the mirror without having to stand up. He sits straight again, with it in his lap.

I meet his eyes with my good one. The bad one is still covered with something that's supposed to be helping it heal. Suddenly my heart is pounding way too hard.

"How bad is it?" I ask him. I tried asking Kara but I don't trust her answer.

It's only when Daniel lets his gaze run over the right side of my face that I realize just how carefully he's been meeting my eye all the time and *not* looking.

"Well," he says, "it looks pretty much like you got badly burned, I suppose. Red and a bit lumpy. And a half-healed gash across your cheek. I suppose the really squeamish might yelp, but I think it could be worse. It's not, like, raw craters or anything horrific like that."

It's not? That's what I've been picturing. *Margaret, help! Don't let me flip out again. Don't let it be too bad!* "Show me."

Daniel pauses—praying?—then holds the mirror up, moving it into position.

Red and lumpy. He's right. All down my head—which is red and half-bald on that side—and trailing down the side of my neck. It comes to within an inch of my nose. Most of my mouth is okay; that's why I can talk relatively pain-free, I suppose. My eye is hidden under the little patch. But...it's *not* raw craters. It's bad. But it's not actually as bad as I thought it might be.

I let out a long breath. "Well, I guess I won't be getting married. But it could be worse."

"Don't talk rubbish," snaps Daniel. "There's no reason you can't marry!"

I blink. *Deja vu.* That's almost exactly what I said to Margaret. I thought she was being silly, saying what she said. Am *I* being silly?

"You can't deny it's super-ugly."

"So what? You shouldn't get married for what's on the outside. Only what's on the inside. A girl who'd worry about that isn't a girl you'd want to marry anyway."

"You saying I've got a built-in gold-digger deflector?"

He grins. "Something like that. Some lovely girl who's absolutely beautiful on the inside just like Saint Margaret will sweep you off your feet one day, you wait and see."

"Wheel me off, more like," I mutter. But my heart lifts, regardless.

CHAPTER 14

Kara reads to me how Margaret threw herself into her new life as a *Mantellata*. Just as, when a child in her cell, she took on a strict program of prayer and mortification, so she did then. Having, it would seem, learned the entire one hundred and fifty psalms by heart from the Holy Spirit, she recited them regularly, along with the Office of the Blessed Virgin and the Office of the Holy Cross (I make a mental note to see if Daniel knows what those are). And she went to hear Mass every single day, and to confession first.

She also meditated a lot, especially on the Incarnation and Nativity. Apparently she absolutely adored contemplating the all-powerful God coming to us as a helpless baby, putting himself entirely in the hands of two mere mortals, Mary and Joseph.

I get that, actually. I mean, the thought that God would voluntarily make Himself that vulnerable, that

He, the one person—people—whatever—who didn't need to have His heart hostage to parental whims, that He should choose it anyway...is incredible.

Not that it's only children who get their hearts messed with. Kara and Llewellyn are trying *so* hard to get me to interact with them again, to talk, to do a crossword or game or look at Llewellyn's new farming magazine or… They try and try and every time I turn my head away and say I'm tired, refusing to engage, well, I don't need to be looking at them to sense their anguish.

It's not *fair*. Why do they have to make me feel so bad for them when they're going to be *giving me back?* I have to stop caring. I have to! I wish Margaret could give me some tips on how to stop loving them, but everything she did was to help herself love God and neighbor *more*.

For example, Margaret faithfully attended the lectures given to the *Mantellate* by the Dominican friars. At one of these, she learned more about Saint Dominic and his regime of prayer and mortification—far stricter than hers. It made such an impression on her that she became convinced that she, a young, unmarried woman with no family, should not be taking advantage of the lighter rules that bound the other *Mantellate*. She began to imitate Saint Dominic far more closely, staying up for much of every night in prayer and meditation and even using the 'discipline.'

"It would certainly take a whip to keep *me* awake at night these days," says Daniel, glumly. "I can't even keep awake all *day*."

Apparently, some of her friends thought she was far too strict with herself and urged her to be satisfied with the trials nature had already given her—her deformities and her parents. But she wouldn't hear of it. She was too generous to give anything but her uttermost in any cause and, to save souls, she would hold back nothing.

One of the main activities of the *Mantellate* was to visit the sick, the poor, and the dying. Day and night, Margaret would limp forth with food or medicine or simple care and encouragement. Only the most hardened sinner, lying upon a deathbed with Margaret at his or her side, could resist her entreaties to turn back to God with love and remorse. As often as not, thanks to Margaret, a person would die at peace with the Creator.

"A beautiful gift," murmurs Daniel, and I'm not sure if he means the peaceful deaths or Margaret's way with the dying.

"Did you know," he tells me, another day, "Saint Margaret was one of the people who did a lot to spread awareness of Saint Joseph? Until the end of the fourteenth century, there wasn't actually a lot of popular devotion to him."

"Yes, it said in the book that Margaret would talk about him to anyone who would listen—for as long as they would listen," I laugh. "I don't actually know a lot about him though."

So Daniel tells me all about Saint Joseph. And Saint Dominic. He knows a lot about religious stuff. No wonder Father Thomas likes him. Or maybe he knows stuff because Father Thomas likes him. I bet Margaret would like him too. Maybe they'll be hanging out together in heaven while I'm still lying in my care home, rotting.

The thought drops me into such a black pit of gloom that I spend the rest of that visit trying to tear Daniel's head off with my tongue. But he comes back the next day, acting like nothing happened, and reads me some more of the book. He really *is* a bit like Margaret.

Margaret goes to live with another well-to-do family, in the rather misnamed 'House of Peace.' The Offrenducci and Macreti families live there, but all is not peaceful. Margaret soon makes things worse by befriending the only daughter of Messer Macreti. She kindles a deep faith in the sixteen-year-old girl, Francesca, or 'Ceccha,' who until then had not been to confession since she was a child and had even forgotten how to go about it. All well and good, until Ceccha decided she did not want to marry as her parents expected her too, but that she wanted to become a *Mantellata*, just like Margaret.

Margaret, who, one day, in the presence of guests, no less, tackled Ceccha's father on the subject. He announced that Ceccha would never wear the habit of a religious, to which Margaret imperturbably stated that before long both Ceccha and her mother Ysachina would be *Mantellata* and wear the Dominican habit for life. Everyone present laughed uproarously, for Ysachina was a very worldly woman who very rarely darkened a church door.

But several months later, Messer Macreti died after a brief, sudden illness. Grief-stricken, his wife turned to God and sought to enter the Order of Penance of St Dominic with her daughter Ceccha. Ceccha was, of course, too young, but the prior, Fra Luigi, who had heard of Margaret's prophecy, concluded that it must therefore be the will of God. And so a second—or rather, third—young woman was admitted.

"See," comments Daniel. "Lay Dominican trailblazer."

Margaret made a second prophecy, about a young man who had been arrested for supporting the wrong political party and who was expected to be condemned and given a harsh penalty. Margaret comforted his mother, declaring that no harm would come to the young man or any fine even be handed out. And to everyone's great surprise, this was the case.

At some point, probably after the death of Messer Macreti, Margaret went to live with the Venturino family instead. In a *palace*.

"Seriously?"

"That's what is says." Daniel places a fingertip to the page. "*Palace.*"

"Wow. So she's come full circle. Raised in a castle and a palace, and now she's in a palace again."

"Yep."

The door opens and Father Thomas looks in. "Ready when you are, Daniel."

Daniel places the bookmark carefully in the book and lays it on the bedside table. "I'd better go, Miri, if you don't mind the cliffhanger too much. It's so nice to get home and settled before I start puking."

"Of course. Thanks for reading."

Daniel waves this away, and moves slowly towards the door. Father Thomas takes his arm as they move away. He seems to be getting more and more tired, dark circles under his eyes. I hope he finishes his treatment before it finishes *him*. Then again, he won't have any reason to come to the hospital then, will he?

+

Palace or not, Margaret insisted on living in a tiny attic room, finding the large guest chamber she'd originally been given too luxurious. After initially refusing her request to move to such uncomfortable quarters, Lord Venturino overheard her correcting his sons' lessons in diverse subjects such as logic, geometry, astronomy, music, and even Latin grammar. Since she could not read and had never had a tutor, he deduced she had the knowledge from the same source as she had learned the psalms—the Holy Spirit. After that, he was not prepared to refuse her anything, so she moved to the simple little room she craved.

Lord Venturino not only took Margaret in, even allowing his guest to live in his garret—a big deal for a proud nobleman—but he also gave permission for Margaret and his wife to visit the prisoners in the jail—the foulest hole in the city, something she desperately wanted to do.

From then on, Margaret, Lady Gregoria Venturino, and some of the other *Mantellate* regularly took food and other necessities to these unfortunates—it sounds as though being in prison in those days was a really bum deal, even if you'd done something quite bad to deserve it. But the best thing the women gave them was dignity, treating them like real people, made in the image and likeness of God.

"That's why you don't kill people," says Daniel firmly. "It doesn't matter how sick they are, you don't give up on them, and you don't kill them. Jesus is in every one of us."

I know he's talking about what the cleaners said—I told him about it, the other day. And yeah, he's talking about some of the things I've said, too, in my bleaker moments, though I've pretty much given up any hope that I might actually die, by now. I keep getting stronger.

So I just say, "What if it's what they want?"

"No can do. Your human dignity doesn't disappear just because *you're* having trouble seeing it at that moment. Truth remains truth, you know. You need to help someone see it, not support their delusion."

"Well, thank you very much!"

But he shrugs, unrepentantly. "If Margaret had got all depressed at some point and decided her life was worthless and of no use to anyone, would it have been true just because she believed it?"

"Of course not!"

"Well, then. It applies to you too, Miri."

CHAPTER 15

One day in the winter, the palace of Venturino caught fire. Able-bodied men ran from all over the city to help fight the flames, but it soon became clear that the house would be lost, and all the attention began to turn to preventing the blaze spreading to other buildings—a serious danger in a crowded medieval city.

Only then did Lady Gregoria realize that Margaret was still in her little garret room at the very top of the house. She rushed like a madwoman towards the burning building, intending to go inside, but men caught her and held her, certain she would die. Beside herself with terror, Gregoria screamed for Margaret to come downstairs quickly, for the house was on fire!

Her prayers interrupted, Margaret came to the head of the stairs, clearly visible above the raging flames. With a few words of reassurance to Gregoria and an entreaty to trust in God, she tossed down her black

Mantellate cloak, telling them to cast it upon the fire. And with that, she went back into her room to resume her prayers. Gregoria did as instructed—and the fire was put out at once.

"Do you think it really happened like that?" I ask Daniel, torn between awe and disbelief.

"Maybe. Many great saints have performed amazing miracles. No one would have taken it for a miracle if they'd just tossed a cloak over a little blaze. People had a lot of experience of fire in those days, remember. They lived cheek to jowl with it. Not like us today. If medieval people say there was a fire serious enough that it should not have been able to be smothered by a cloak, then I'll believe them. People like to think folks in olden times were thick and gullible, but sometimes I think it's us who're thick."

I'm still turning it in my mind when I realize Daniel's fallen asleep with his head on the bed. Oh well. I'd like to hear more of the book, but I'm not going to wake him. He's so zonked, these days.

My mind returns to the miracle, my namesake. How much faith would you need to be so calm in that situation? To act like you literally knew it was all going to be okay—because you did? That level of faith just fills me with...with awe...

+

Stripe stops, ears flicking, snorting. What? There's a strange noise, a clanking-revving-crashing-undulating, louder and louder and —

I look around. A red tractor and hay baler is rolling — rolling side over side, like a rolling pin! — down the hill straight towards me. Time seems to slow — I start to press my heels to Stripe — the tractor bounces, smashing through the last hedge —

Stripe rears up —

And it hits.

The impact is terrible. Stripe slams backwards into me — we're falling. I hit the ground so hard. I don't know what's happening. Pain hammers through me — Stripe's screaming, my cheek's all wet, where it lies on the grass. Bleeding? A sickly smell sears my nostrils, is it diesel?

I can't see properly. I want to help Stripe, but I can't see and I can't move and I don't understand what's happening.

I lie, panting in pain, as my vision grays in and out. In and out. Finally, I begin to understand. The things close to my face are the tines of an upside down hay baler. The tractor...it hit us. I'm hurt. I must be hurt. Hurt bad. So is Stripe. Is he lying on my legs? We need help.

But I can't see. I can't move. I try to look around but I can barely do more than rotate one eye. What's that? My book lies on the grass, the pages fluttering. A line drawing fills my vision, of a little bent-over lady, hobbling along with a crutch. Saint Margaret of Castello.

"Saint Margaret, help!" I more mouth the words than whisper them, because everything hurts so much and I can barely seem to breathe.

Everything's so quiet, except Stripe's low groans. Even the wheels on the hay baler have stopped spinning now, up there in the air above me. I'm going to die here, all alone. Unwanted as ever. No! Please, no!

Saint Margaret, help me! Help us! Please, save me and...and I promise I'll take your name. Even though you're a girl. I promise! Just save me...please?

A gentle breeze caresses my face, cool over my damp cheek. A soft 'whump' sound comes from the tractor. What's that?

Smoke. I smell smoke. I twist my head, trying to see...but I can't really move. Soon I can see the flames, though, licking over the tractor, running along the grass towards the hay baler. Towards me.

I can't stop them. I cannot stop them.

I can barely even scream.

CHAPTER 16

"Margaret!" I wake with a yell.

"Huh?" Daniel starts awake too, raising his head from the bed, the book sticking to his cheek for a moment before dropping off.

"Margaret! She started the fire!"

"What? Are you okay, Miri? You look—"

"I thought I didn't remember the accident. I thought I passed out when it hit us. But I didn't! I remember—I remember everything…I was going to die, all alone…I begged Margaret to help…and the tractor caught fire. Kara said it was a miracle a diesel tractor caught fire like that—and if it hadn't, I'd have been dead before they even missed me. Margaret did it! That's why she said we'd sort of met already!"

Daniel, squinting and rubbing his eyes sleepily, is clearly making a big effort to try and follow all this. "Are you saying Margaret saved you by setting fire to a tractor?"

"Yes. But it had leaked diesel and my head was lying in it. Kara and Llewellyn didn't quite get to me in time. But I did survive. Which is what I asked her for."

"Wow," Daniel stares at me. "That's...are you okay? You really do look rather..."

My insides are churning, like they've turned to jelly and someone's shaking it back and forth and pulverizing it. I can't catch my breath properly. In my head I'm lying there in that diesel-soaked grass, dying, alone, lying there, watching the flames coming, lying there... My throat's so tight and my eye pricks fiercely. No. Miracle Taylor never cries. Never. Never cries...

"What's that you're saying?" asks Daniel worriedly.

Heck, I'm whispering it out loud as I fight to control myself.

"Miri?" Daniel reaches out and grips my shoulder, one of the few places where nothing is broken or pinned. "Have you seen the Lord of the Rings?"

"What?" I whisper. I can barely speak, my voice vibrating and cracking as the tears try to overwhelm me.

"Have you?"

"Of course."

"Well, who is the manliest man in it?"

Manliest man? I can't think. "I dunno. Boromir?" He has a really big sword and shield, right?

Daniel winces in a pained manner. "*Boromir?*"

"Uh..." Maybe answering his dumb questions will keep my mind off...I struggle to think. "Okay, okay, *Aragorn*."

"Exactly. And when Boromir dies, what does Aragorn do?"

I try to picture the scene, try to picture anything but grass, lonely death, unwantedness, flames...and I know what Daniel's getting at it. I don't want to say it—but I kind of do.

"He...he cries."

"Yes. Aragorn, the manliest man that ever manned up and did, cries. Please let it out, Miri. It's okay to cry."

And I can't, I just can't hold it back. Not while he's saying things like that. Not while he's gripping my shoulder and telling me it's okay. I sob. And sob. And sob. Years and years of tears. I go on so long Daniel's seriously drooping, like holding my shoulder like this is becoming exhausting. It's not as though he can hug me. No one can. I'm a broken mess of bones and a shoulder-grip is the most comfort I can receive.

It doesn't matter. It is good to let it out. When I finally run out of tears—or maybe just energy—I lie staring up at the ceiling while Daniel kinda slumps in the chair.

I promised. I promised Margaret... A week or so back I wasn't even sure I was going to get confirmed. Some moments I was adamant I wasn't, ever. But after spending all this time with Daniel and learning more about Margaret, the idea's been growing on me again. God's been growing on me. The idea that maybe He actually could love me, despite everything.

Now the decision's made for me. I *promised* I'd take her name. So I will. I'm surprised how happy it makes me feel. I think I'm figuring it out, though. God doesn't have arms and a physical voice, so He can't give me a big hug and yell 'I love you, Miracle Taylor' in my ear. So He sends people like Daniel and Margaret to do it for Him.

+

Daniel doesn't say anything about me crying the next day. He chats normally, like he doesn't think less of me at all, and then offers to read a chapter from the book. We're very near the end, now.

One of Margaret's fellow *Mantellate*, Sister Venturella, was suffering from a tumor in her eye. She went to one of the best physicians available, but he said it was unlikely her sight could be saved. And the fee he would charge for trying was more than she could afford anyway.

Utterly despondent, Sister Venturella went to Margaret for comfort—apparently oblivious, in her self-centered misery, to the fact that bewailing her imminent blindness to one blind from birth was a tad insensitive.

Margaret didn't care about that, though, and listened with love to the sorry tale. But her words of comfort were more of a challenge, and one not to Sister

Venturella's taste. Margaret told her that her imminent blindness was in fact a gift from God—a gift that, should she embrace it, would draw her much closer to him. So passionately did Margaret believe this, that she *begged* Sister Venturella to accept it willingly.

But Sister Venturella could not. She railed against God for being cruel to her. Margaret explained to her that to suffer now was the same as undergoing a painful treatment from a physician. It hurt for a time, but afterwards the benefit was great. To no avail—Sister Venturella was too frightened of being blind. She would rather die, she said—even more insensitively!

Margaret felt Sister Venturella was blind already, in a different way, but since she could not persuade her, she got her friend to put her little hand on her eye—and the tumor was cured at once.

Daniel stops reading at that point, and we sit in silence. What's he thinking? I wish Margaret would put her hand on my face, on my shattered body, and cure it all. But that's not what she'd do first, is it? She'd tell me it was a gift, should I choose to accept it. I sympathize with Sister Venturella, who just wanted to be spared the suffering.

"Does anyone actually believe that sort of thing?" I say at last.

Daniel looks up from what has become more doze than reflection. "What?"

"That some terrible suffering they've been landed

with is a *gift*."

Daniel's silent for quite a while. "I'm not in the habit of thinking of it in quite those terms," he says at last. "But I wouldn't un-wish my leukemia. Which is kind of the same thing, I suppose."

I stare at him, speechless for a moment. "What do you mean, you wouldn't un-wish it? Surely if you could choose to never have become ill, you'd take it?"

Daniel shakes his head. "I don't think so. My life was so empty beforehand. I thought the stupidest things were important. I barely knew God. I had some seriously superficial friendships, some of them. I didn't appreciate life, health, time, anything, not properly. I have been a hundred times more fulfilled, happier, closer to God, since I was forced to take a long hard look at it all and start preparing for the next life. No, I wouldn't give it up."

"Not for...for another six decades of life?"

He shakes his head. "Sixty more empty years are just sixty more wasted years. I'd rather live a few years well than all that time badly."

I don't know what else to say, so I say nothing. Was Margaret right? Can a suffering really be a gift? Somehow it's harder to dismiss now I know a real, live, flesh and blood, sane person who feels that way too. At least, I thought Daniel was sane. Margaret would think I was the mad one, perhaps, for not embracing my ruined life as an express lane to holiness. But it's so *hard*.

It's not just my body, that's the real problem. If it was just that, it would be easier. But I'm going to lose Kara and Llewellyn because of it. And it's very, very hard to forgive God for that—though I am trying. But to *embrace* it?

How, Lord?

CHAPTER 17

I open my eyes to find Margaret—*Saint* Margaret—sitting beside my bed.

"Am I asleep?"

She smiles, her gentle, unfocussed gaze filling the room with love. "Does it matter?"

"I suppose not." I shoot her another look. "Um, thank you for saving me."

She bows her head. "It was God, not I."

"Well, thank you for asking Him to save me."

She can't dodge this thank you, and smiles bashful acceptance.

"I'm going to take your name, like I promised. But, uh, I haven't quite finished the book yet. I can't read it myself because I can't hold it. Kara was talking about finding some sort of stand—but there are pins in the way at the moment, and I can't turn the pages anyway. So people are reading to me." I'm blathering, but I can't help it, I'm so pleased to see her, but kind of in awe, too. I can tell, now, that's she's wearing that Dominican habit-thing. Not just a white dress and a bandanna.

She nods. "That is a great blessing, to you and even more to those who help you."

"More to them?"

Another nod. "They are ministering to Christ in you. Such an honor."

I never ever thought of helping someone else as an *honor*, before.

"So, what happened to you in the end? Did you live a long, happy live in Lord Venturino's palace?"

She smiles. "I always lived a happy life and that continued. But not a long one. I was ever so busy. I kept going to the prison. One prisoner, I remember particularly. He was in the very depths of despair, poor man. He had lost everything. It is hard to even narrate to you his story. His brother had been suspected of treason, but had fled before he could be arrested. The man, Alonzo, was arrested in his place, and he was tortured, of course, as was usual back then, but he could not tell what he did not know. Eventually, they threw him into prison, broken from his torture, and left him there."

"That's awful."

"That was not the worst of it. Because he remained in prison so long, his wife and child lost their home and then his little boy died of starvation, with him utterly unable to help them. He became near-deranged with grief and bitterness, and turned against God with such violence that those who tried to help him fled in terror from his very words. It broke my heart to see him in such a state. I prayed so hard for him—and the Lord used something about me to reach the poor man. The joy of seeing that man reach out to God again, after all that time—" She falls silent, overcome with the memory, eyes glistening with emotion.

"But what happened to you? In the end?"

"To me?" She says it in her sweet way, as though it is of little importance. "Why, I grew sick, this twisted little body of mine not being very strong, and I found a permanent home at last—with God."

"You died?" Well, that's disappointing. "How old were you?

"Thirty-three. The same age as my Lord, an honor of which I was wholly undeserving." She cocks her head, as though able to sense my dismay. "Did you expect some grander fate? Marriage to a prince? A gory martyrdom, perhaps?" A twinkle of humor gleams in her eye.

"I...don't know what I expected, actually. It still makes me sad."

"Don't be. In all honesty, though I ignored it as much as I could so that I might serve others, my physical sufferings were not inconsiderable, all my life long. And by then, my soul craved my Lord as a man in the desert craves water. The Dominican monks processed to the Venturino palace—as an honor guard for the Blessed Sacrament, you see—and I was able to receive Holy Communion to speed me on my way. I could never physically see Our Lord in the Blessed Sacrament, of course, yet during every Mass, from Consecration to Communion I could always *see* Him and I do not merely mean a vision or imagining—I never could quite explain it to anyone. *Infinite Beauty…*"

She trails off, lost for a moment in a joy I can only envy. Then she brings her attention back to me with a little shake of her head. "Well, it was during Eastertime, a season of joy. It was not a sad death."

Not a sad death. Here was me not aware there was any other kind.

"And you became a saint? How?"

"Well, by arriving in God's presence to behold His infinite beauty forever, I became a saint. But my official recognition by the Church took a lot longer. As a *Mantellata*, I was able to claim the privilege of being laid to rest in the Dominican church, instead of the parish church and, in accordance with my wishes, my body was washed and wrapped in my black cloak, and carried on a bier to the Chiesa della Carita. An extraordinary number of people followed along behind." She adds that in a rather puzzled way, as though she can't imagine why.

"After the funeral rites, the friars tried to carry my

body out to the cloister for burial, but the townspeople grew very agitated, insisting that I should be buried in the church itself, where they would have access to me. It turned into quite an uproar, almost a riot. The friars did not know what to do. They tried to insist that I should be buried in the cloister until the Church actually proclaimed me a saint, but the townspeople knew well enough that few if any of them could possibly hope to live to see that day, and refused to give way.

"Then a man and his wife carried their young mute and crippled daughter through the crowd to where my body lay. In pity for them, everyone began to implore God that she should be healed, as did I. And she was."

"A little girl got healed at your funeral?"

"She did. Perhaps fortunately, for it settled the argument and quelled the imminent riot. I was laid to rest in the church, after all. My mortal body still lies near that spot in a newer church, the Chiesa di San Domenico, awaiting the return of my soul on the last day. You may see me, in fact, for I am in a good state of preservation, a little browned by time but essentially incorrupt, and have been laid in a glass coffin. It pleased the good Lord to have it so. People still go there seeking healing."

"So when were you actually *declared* a saint?"

"The Black Death distracted everyone from little unimportant me. And then there was war after war." She sighs, heavily, as though at the memory of each conflict. "Well, in 1609, Pope Paul V beatified me on the nineteenth of October and named the thirteenth of April as my...my feast day." Margaret bows her head again, her cheeks reddening. "Though I am unworthy of such an honor. And then in 2021, as another, thankfully lesser, plague raged, Pope Francis canonized me. It was only then, after all those years, that I *officially* became a saint. Certainly there was no reason for anyone to rush, over *me*. I am glad they did not."

"Have you done any miracles recently? Daniel said something about you and *two hundred* miracles?"

She bows her head again, blushing, and does not answer.

"But wasn't there a special miracle before you were canonized?" I'm sure Daniel mentioned something about that sort of thing for saints.

"Usually there is, but I was canonized by a different process. It's called 'equipollent'—that means equivalent—canonization and it doesn't revolve around any one, specific, miracle. It's when, instead of the Church introducing a new saint to everyone, the Church recognizes as a saint someone who is already largely functioning as one in the life of the Church. Someone with a very long-running reputation for miracles, sanctity, and people's devotion. Really," her eyes glint with humor, "it's a bit like the Church saying, 'Oh, yes, this one slipped down the cracks, but yes, you are all quite correct, she is indeed a saint.'"

"Daniel said you used to *levitate*. Is that true?"

She blushes even more. "I know nothing of it, except what was reported to me by reliable eye-witnesses. Since I must either accept their word or believe that every one of them perjured him or herself, then yes, it would seem I used to do such a thing. It seemed to be a regular occurrence at the prison. I think the misery of those poor souls drove me to new heights of prayer—literally, it would seem." Her eyes twinkle. Yes, the book said she had a cheerful disposition and lively sense of humor—though of course, I already knew that!

I think for a while. "So, if I came to your tomb? Might I be healed?"

Her face falls. Yep, she's disappointed. "I would pray for you and, if it pleased the Lord, of course you might be. I cannot say. But there is far more important healing you should seek first."

My heart and soul. In this—dream?—state I am unable to pretend, even to myself, that I do not understand what she means.

I don't want to let go the idea of physical healing. And yet... "Then, dear Margaret, will you pray for my heart and soul to be healed?"

Her ugly face is made beautiful by her radiant smile. "Of *course* I will, *caro* Miri."

When I open my eye, the sounds from the corridor say nighttime, but Kara sits by the bed, stroking my forehead, Margaret's book forgotten in her hand, as though she has been reading from it. "Miri? Miri, are you properly awake? Llewey, he's awake!"

"I'll get the nurse!" Llewey's quick steps tread to the door.

"What's happening?" My voice is slurred with sleep.

"You came down with a bit of an infection. Your temperature went very high. But they hooked you up to some intravenous antibiotics and we've been waiting for you to pull around. Oh Miri, I'm so glad to see that brown eye of yours looking up at me!"

I smile back at her, basking in her smile. Until I remember...

My smile fades.

Her face falls. "Oh, Miri. I don't understand what we've done." Her face catches slightly. "Please tell us what we've done? Why you don't like us anymore. I..." her face...wobbles, "I'm so sorry we didn't get there sooner. We really did come as fast as we could. Maybe if we'd been even a few moments quicker...maybe you wouldn't have been burned *quite* so badly. I don't know. Oh, Miri, I'm *so sorry*..."

I stare at her, trying to process what she's saying. My mind feels thick, as though it's full of syrup. Why is she apologizing for that? It's not what they've done, it's what they're going to do.

"And now you look so puzzled. Oh, lamb, I'm sorry

to go on about all this when you've been so sick. I'll stop."

"I'm not angry with you." Talking is tiring. I really have been ill again.

"You're not?"

"No."

"Then why don't you like us anymore?"

"I *do*," the words are out before I can stop them. "Very much. I'm just...*trying not to*. Because it will be easier."

"Easier?"

"When you give me back. And get the new kid, the one who can work on the farm." My head aches. It swims. I close my eye again. No, I've not been well. Not at all.

The nurse bustles in. I keep my eye closed. I'm too tired. I can sense her checking all the monitors and making happy sounds. I must be recovering. Good. No need to stay awake, then...

CHAPTER 18

Daniel and I are still discussing my dream about Margaret five days later. I'm trying to ignore the fact that Daniel's chemo will finish tomorrow and he won't be here several days a week any more. I'm going to miss him so much. Maybe he can come to visit me anyway. But he looks like he needs to lie down and crash out for a week or two.

"So what I'm thinking is," I tell Daniel, "If God wants to cure me, He will. And I'll be really grateful. But maybe I'm not going to run around after it, like it's more important than anything else. I'm going to concentrate on getting to know God first of all. That's the big thing. Otherwise I'll feel like I'm just, I don't know, *using* Him and Margaret for physical healing. Or trying to."

Daniel smiles. "I think your friend's wisdom is rubbing off on you."

"What, yours?" I tease.

His cheeks go red. "I meant Saint Margaret's!"

"Sure you did."

"Ugh, you little menace. You knew what I meant."

"Did I?"

We're still laughing when Kara and Llewellyn come in. Llewellyn's here? I thought he'd had to go back to the farm again? But before my heart can lift, I see the two strangers with them, a man and a woman. Everything about them makes me think: social workers.

The amusement drains from me like ice-cold water. Is it happening? Now? Before I'm even out of hospital? But it could be weeks before I'm out of here. Months, even. They can't stay with me all that time, the farm will go to ruin. I suppose it makes far better sense for them to make the break quickly. Then I'm not their problem anymore and they can go back to Wales and leave me to Social Services.

A huge lump wedges itself in my throat, but I don't care what Daniel says, I'm not crying in front of them. Not now.

"Oh, hello, Daniel," says Kara. "Sorry to disturb you, but we need to talk to Miri."

"That's okay, Mrs. Mann. I'll go."

Daniel squeezes my shoulder and leaves.

I stare at the ceiling, still fighting with that lump in my throat.

"Miri?" The male social worker has come to the side

of the bed. "I understand this is all rather sudden, but Mr. and Mrs. Mann got in touch with us because they felt that just at the moment you would benefit very much from greater stability in your life. We agree, so we're happy for everything to go through very quickly. We're hoping to sign the papers right now, if you're happy."

"Since when does it matter what I think?" I whisper. *I will not cry. I will not.*

"Well, strictly speaking, we can go ahead without your consent. But of course, at your age, it's better to involve you in the process."

"Miri," says the lady social worker, "we know you're very ill and we don't want to put pressure on you. But we're a little concerned that you don't seem happy. We were given to understand that you wanted the adoption to take place."

I blink at the ceiling. I replay what she just said. I turn my head so sharply that quite a few not-yet-completely-knitted bones lower down my body say ouch. Or OUCH.

"*What* did you say?"

"Mr. and Mrs. Mann would like to sign the adoption papers. Today. I know we weren't planning to finalize things just yet, but in the circumstances we agree that it—"

"Let me see them! The papers!" *Is it, can it be, could it be, possibly be...true?*

With a puzzled air, the man takes a handful of printed papers from a folder and holds them in front of me. He's not very practiced at it and they waver as he tries not to stare at my burned face and gets the distance totally wrong. I peer frantically at them, trying to make out the words.

They are. I think they really are. Will they really— Is this some horrible joke? One last horrible joke on me, Miri the unwanted?

"Sign them!" I stare wildly at Kara and Llewellyn. "If you really mean it, sign them!"

"You consent?" says the man.

"*Yes*. Sign them, *please?*"

Is it real, is it true, is it good, is it beautiful, is it really going to happen, is it, is it, isitisitisit...?

In agonizing slow motion, the man lays the papers out on the bedside table. Kara and Llewellyn join him. They talk and point and sign here and there. It takes fifty million years and I count every second.

But finally...

...it's done.

"Look, Miri," says Kara, holding the paper up properly this time, so I can read it.

Adoption...my name...their names...signatures...it's done.

I burst into tears. I cry so hard I'm afraid they'll fetch a nurse with a sedative. But Llewellyn—my dad— simply squeezes my shoulder while Kara—my mum—

strokes my hair, on and on. The social workers smile and slip away.

"Oh, Miri," whispers Kara—Mum—as she tries to soothe me. "We told you so many times. But after what you said the other day, we realized this might be the only way you'd ever believe it."

"You were right," I blurt—then I'm crying again.

Eventually my sobs finally trail off and I manage to sniff, "But how will you manage?" I look at my new dad. "You said there was no room for slackers in a farming family."

"Oh, Miri! You silly boy!" He squeezes my shoulder yet again. "Don't you understand what a slacker is? A slacker is someone who doesn't do something they *could* and should do. If you never do another chore again, because of *this*," he waves down my pin-cushion body, "you'll never count as a *slacker*. When I said that, Miri, it was because I wanted so much for you to get *involved*. A farm is like an extra family member, it can never be ignored, always needs attention. If you couldn't learn to love the farm too, we were going to have a problem. But you don't put someone out of your family for something like *this*. It can happen to anyone."

"But I'm going to take up so much of your time," I whisper. Have they done the right thing? Am I being selfish?

"Miri, Llewey's right," says my new mum, "you are being silly. Of course you will need a lot of help, especially to begin with. However long, it doesn't matter. We will just find a new routine. The government will help a bit financially, you know, and there are charities that will help too, with the things you need. And I bet you'll find *something* you can do to help, if you're the slightest bit able. And if you can't, then it *doesn't matter*, okay? *Can't do* and *won't do* are very different things. So no more worrying about it, young Mr. Miracle Mann."

She shows me the paper again. "See, it's official. You have the best name in the history of names. Miracle Mann. Look, there it is."

We all laugh. Yeah, that was always the drawback with them adopting me. But I don't care. I have a mum and dad. Real and alive, and they like me, scars and pins and all. They *love* me. Kara—Mum—is kissing my forehead yet again.

Mum. My mum.

At last.

CHAPTER 19

"Miracle Mann?" A grin splits Daniel's face. "Oh *man*, I hadn't thought it through. I don't know whether to laugh my head off or say heck, that's awesome. Can I do both?"

"Do whatever you like. I don't care. I am so happy, I'm full of helium. I don't need to be able to walk. I shall just float around, everywhere, forever."

"Well, Miracle Mann does sound like someone with superpowers."

I snort. "Ah, it doesn't matter. Soon I'll be Miracle Margaret Mann. Am I ever glad I don't have to go to school again! Miracle Mann and a girl's name. I'd never have a moment's peace ever again and I didn't get much before."

"You don't have to use your confirmation name in daily life. Unless you want to."

"I feel like I should. Since she helped save my life

and everything."

"Well, MMM are cool initials, right?"

"*I* think so."

But when we finally stop laughing and joking, Daniel looks more serious. He pulls out a piece of paper. "Look, I've had my last session, now. My mum won't let me come here again for a while, no way. Not until my immunity is back up. And you said they're talking about transferring you to a Welsh hospital in another month. So I don't know if I'll be able to come and see you before you go. I will try, but my mum can get so nervous."

He holds the paper in front of my eyes. "Here is my phone number, email address, and address, okay? You should be able to talk to me on the phone sometime, at least. Hopefully you can email too, once your fingers have healed and the physical therapists have done with you. I mean, all you have to do is poke the keys one by one."

I swallow a lump in my throat. I wish he could still come and see me, but I am happy for him, that his treatment is over. No more puking. No more leukemia—at least for a while. Though I hope he's wrong about...*that*.

"Hold it there for a moment," I say. "I want to memorize your number. Stuff gets lost in hospitals."

"Doesn't it just. But if you do forget or lose the paper, just email Father Thomas via the church website."

"Good idea." But I still stare at that number until I think I've drilled it into my mind and only then let him put the paper safe(ish) in the bedside drawer.

"D'you want to say a rosary?" he asks.

"Okay."

I pray for him. I think he's praying for me.

All too soon, Father Thomas is opening the door. Daniel gives my shoulder a squeeze and walks away, thin and tired.

I really, really, really hope he's wrong.

+

After months in hospital, just sitting in a car and seeing the world whirling by is exhilarating and exhausting all at once. They moved me back to Wales in an ambulance several months ago, and I didn't really see anything. Hardly any windows and I was so wiped out by the time they even got me into it, I slept for most of the journey.

By the time we reach the farm, I'm asleep this time, as well. When Kara wakes me gently, we're already stopped in the yard. Four sheepdogs are crowding around the door, tails wagging, while one hangs back, growling slightly.

"Get on with you, Owl." Llewellyn shoos grumpy old Owl away, then goes back to setting up the wheelchair. Being lifted out of the car is very painful, though I try not to show it. Partly because I don't want to upset Dad-L, as I call him, and partly because I'm trying to offer all my pains for Daniel.

Once I'm settled in the chair, in the special foam thing that supports my misshapen body, and the pain has receded a little, I'm able to look around. The farmyard looks much the same, just less tidy. Except...

"What is that?" Something stands outside the workshop.

"Ah, that." I can tell Dad-L is pleased I noticed because he wants to show it off.

"Oh, come on, that can wait," says Mum. "He needs to rest."

"No, I'm okay for a few more minutes," I say quickly. "I'd like to see what it is."

Dad-L wheels me closer. Wheels, long shafts...

"Is it a...a horse cart?"

"Technically, it's a pony trap. But basically, a small cart, yes."

A little tendril of hope uncoils in my heart. "Whose...uh...is it?"

"It's yours. I asked Mr. E's son if we could buy it, but he gave it to you."

"I, um, don't have a pony." A stab of pain dissipates the tendril somewhat. Poor brave Stripe...

"Nor a body that's up to bouncing in a trap, either," says Dad-L, "so I think we've got some time to worry about the pony problem. And the cart needs work. I was hoping to have it done up a bit better before you got home, but I've been too busy."

There's a lot of rust and peeling paint. But still... As Dad-L wheels me into the house and gets me into bed, I'm hardly thinking about the pain. My mind is full of pony traps...and living, breathing ponies with soft noses and flicking ears.

CHAPTER 20

7 MONTHS LATER

"Walk on," I call, speaking clearly.

Maggie steps out smartly along the track. I hold the reins loosely in my twisted hands, but only so I can make the tiniest contact with her mouth to tell her whether I mean left or right when I shout directions. She only gets 'left' and 'right' correct about eighty percent of the time, without the help. She's a very smart pony, though. She had some extra training from the support ponies' charity before coming to me. She knows loads of commands, most verbal.

I've only been able to drive her out by myself for a few weeks and it's still bliss to be bowling along, by myself, the wind in my hair, the rugged crucifix Daniel sent for my confirmation bouncing on my chest, my clever little pony up front with her two eyes. My bad eye is still a dead loss, but I don't need a license for this. Maggie can see depth for both of us.

I've come further than I have before, all the way to the farm at the bottom of the valley. The junction with the proper road is coming up in another quarter mile. I can't go further than that. I promised Mum and Dad-L. I'll turn in a field gateway when I get there and head back.

But as we approach the start of this farm's drive, there's a girl standing there, watching me. About my age? Or slightly younger? Hard to tell.

"Whoa, Maggie." Obediently, Maggie clops to a neat halt, without me needing to hurt my hands trying to pull too hard on the reins. "Good girl. Stand."

I free a hand and press the little electric button that activates the trap's powerful brakes. Just in case something does spook Maggie, despite her blinkers and all that training. Dad-L has done so much to my trap, to make it possible for me to use it as safely as possible. I'm *so* grateful they've resisted the temptation to wrap me in cotton wool, now I'm so very breakable, and are letting me do what I can do. I'm even starting to find a few things I can do to help the farm—though it *is* difficult with my bad hands.

The girl walks up and, too late, I remember my face. I haven't seen anyone I don't know for so long, I'd actually forgotten it for a moment. Bother. Why did I stop?

She stands beside the front wheels, staring openly at me without a trace of embarrassment. Her face is odd, somehow, round and with strange eyes.

"Hi," she says, in a slightly nasal voice. "I'm Annie. Who are you?"

"I'm Miri." Oh, why did I stop!

"What's wrong with your face?"

Heat rushes into my disaster-story of a mug. I gesture towards the left side with my claw-like hand. "Mankind happened. Someone did that on purpose." I gesture to the other side. "And that by accident." Then, because I'm mad at her for being so rude, I demand, "What's wrong with *yours?*"

Her face falls. "God made me this way. I have Down's Syndrome."

Down's Syndrome? My face heats up in shame, now. Heck, how couldn't I see that? I suppose I associate Down's Syndrome with slow-witted kids getting pushed around in gloomy city schools, not with a cheerful girl out by herself in the countryside.

"I'm sorry," I say. "I was rude."

She stares at me thoughtfully. "Was *I* rude? I didn't mean to be rude, but maybe I was rude too."

"It doesn't matter. My face is a mess."

She studies me all over again. "Well, it's *interesting*," she announces, finally. "You do not have a boring face. I expect people at school call you Scarface, though."

Seriously? "What do they call you, Moonface?"

She nods, missing my sarcasm. "Yes. I don't really mind, though. Or I try not to. Think about it, when people look up and see the moon, they're like, *Ooh, beautiful, it's the moon*. So when they call me Moonface, it's like they're calling me Beautiful Face. Even if they don't realize they are. It doesn't sound very tough, though. Scarface is a really tough nickname. Like a pirate. Sometimes I just go up to people and say, *I'm Moonface*. And then they can't do anything. Because I stole the name from them. You should do that. Just say, *Hi, I'm Scarface*. That will sort them out, you'll see."

My turn to stare at her. It's not such a bad idea. And I don't actually think she's trying to be rude at all. She's just super-direct. I need to stop snapping at her. "Uh, good idea. Though I don't actually go to school anymore. I'm homeschooled."

"Oh, that's nice. Mum homeschooled me for a while when we first came here, but she didn't like it. I have to go to school again now." She sounds glum about it.

"That's a shame."

"Yeah." She sighs. "I like your pony. I'd love to pet her but she's got that sign on her."

She can read...why should I be surprised? She talks pretty much like anyone her age—practically my age, I think. She just seems a bit more frank and open and enthusiastic. Thirteen with no filter.

She reads the words from the fluorescent stripes on Maggie's harness out loud. "*Please do not distract me, I am working. Assistance Pony*. Is she very special?"

"Yes. It's, uh, hard for me to do much."

Embarrassed, I make a slight gesture to my crooked body, nestled in its supportive custom foam seat liner. "But Maggie lets me do more."

She cost even more than Stripe—all those brains—but the pony charity and several of the neighbors paid for her. I'm still bowled away by that.

"That's lovely." She still eyes Maggie admiringly.

Unexpectedly, I'm actually enjoying meeting this girl.

"I'm uh, just going along to the main road and turning around. Do you want a ride?"

Her eyes go wide. "Ooh, yes, please. I should check with Mum..." she glances over her shoulder at the distant farmhouse "...when I get back. Then you can come in for some tea."

She climbs eagerly up to sit beside me as I hide a smile.

"What's that inside your jacket?" I ask.

It's a sleepy lamb. She introduces me to the cute orphan, then I tell Maggie to walk on, and off we go.

When we get back to her farmhouse, her mother appears at the door at the clop of hooves. Another, younger woman peers from the barn.

"This is my mum," chatters Annie. "And that's Jess, the lamber. Mum, can Miri come in for some tea?"

"Uh..." Annie's mum eyes me in confusion, taking in Maggie's warning labels and all the hi-tech additions to the trap. No doubt she's heard something about me—

small valley, after all. "He *may*, but can he?"

Annie looks confused, but I understand. "I can, if I may," I say, trying to smile, hideously self-conscious under the eyes of the two strange grown-ups. Well, Jess—who smiles and nods at me—looks slightly familiar from before my accident, though I don't think I've met her since. I've never seen Annie or her mum before, though. When did they move here?

"Welcome, then." Annie's mum tries to smile but only succeeds in looking anxious. "Do you need any help?"

"I'm okay." I activate the brake, then move the lever to turn my padded seat around. Dad-L hasn't worked out how to make that electric yet, so I just have to grit my teeth and push with my hands and feet. Once it's facing sideways I touch the button to drop the ramp Dad-L just built into the rear section of the trap. Until then, he had to lift me in and out—now, I'm fully independent! Good timing, since I've just been invited in for tea.

Then it's merely a question of getting my crutches— specially adapted to put as little force on my hands as possible—properly arranged, levering myself very carefully to my feet and hobble-shuffling even more carefully down the ramp and onto the uneven stone paving of the old farmyard.

Yeah. I can walk now. Sorta-kinda-well enough. Just a very little way. I get to offer up a LOT for Daniel each time I do it, but I don't care. Watch me walk! Okay, shuffle.

Thanks be to God and Saint Margaret.

+

I'm shattered when I get home, but I'm very happy to have met Annie. She was so friendly and straightforward. Which was sometimes slightly awkward, but very refreshing. Nice to have someone nearby who's actually my age, too. Catherine's always very nice to me, but she is several years older and has her own friends. Daniel's older as well, of course, but we boys who chat to dead people have to stick together, don't we?

I take some extra painkillers and tough it out for a while, though I keep my electric wheelchair parked in the corner of the kitchen and don't really move around. But I let Mum talk me into going to bed early. Driving my trap takes it out of me enough, let alone walking in and out of a house. The first time I managed a step—when I knew it really was going to be possible to walk again—I admit it, I cried. So did Dad-L. Walking makes so much difference to being able to do stuff myself.

Just look at today! I couldn't have had tea with Annie if I hadn't been able to walk into the house. There's no way I'll ever get my big wheelchair into the back of my little pony trap. For a while I thought I might be able to have a little folding manual wheelchair in the back, so someone could get me out in that and push me along, but now I don't need to. Not for a few steps, anyway.

Okay, Annie still had to carry my foam support seat in—Daniel would probably live to a hundred, easy-peasy, if I sat without it for even ten minutes, 'cause heck, does it hurt, but I'm under very strict orders from the doctors not to do without it, even if I was brave enough to try. But maybe eventually I'll just be able to put it over my shoulder and carry it myself.

I glance at the wheelchair with its big off-road tires, parked beside the bed in my specially-adapted ground floor bedroom. Will I ever be able to do without it? I doubt it. However much I improve, I can't imagine ever being able to walk around for *hours*, let alone a whole day. And *stairs*... I shudder. But it doesn't matter. To be able to walk a little—just like Margaret—is enough for me.

Tired or not, I lie staring out the window at the stars—and the moon. My life's got so good—despite everything. But I feel a bit like Margaret felt—I should be doing something more. If I'm alive, if I've healed this well, surely there's a reason? Some way I should be serving?

Something Annie said over tea has stuck in my mind. Actually, if felt like it hit me in the forehead with the force of a bullet and lodged deep in my brain. She told me ninety percent of people with Down's Syndrome are killed if it gets diagnosed before they're born—and far more cases are diagnosed than not. That's beyond awful. At least most kids with cleft lip do get born. But kids in the womb as deformed as I am now—as Margaret was at birth—so many of them are simply killed.

Daniel said in his last email he'd been to stand outside an abortion clinic to pray and offer help to women who were going in because they didn't know what else to do. Would Annie want to do something like that with me? We could stand outside together looking happy to be alive, preaching without saying a word, like Saint Francis may or may not (according to Daniel) have actually said to do.

I wonder if Mum and Dad-L would let me. I am pretty breakable, if someone didn't like what we were doing. But what did Daniel say? That he didn't want to hoard his life like a miser. I don't know how long I've got, what problems may arise from all my injuries in the future. I seem okay right now, but there are no guarantees for the long-term, that's what they said. Either way, I don't want to be a miser. I want to do something good. What point is it being alive if I don't?

"Margaret," I murmur, into the darkness, "pray that I'll know if it's the right thing. And help me persuade Mum and Dad-L and Annie's parents, if it is."

My best friend has got my back. And her name is mine.

Yeah, Miracle Margaret Taylor Mann, AKA 'Scarface,' Defender of the Innocent, is ready for action.

Thanks be to God.

DISCUSSION QUESTIONS

1. *Margaret and Miri both suffer several catastrophic events in their young lives, but they react very differently. Margaret continues to believe that God loves her, while Miri concludes that He doesn't.*

- Why do you think they react so differently?
- Whose reaction do you most identify with and why?

2. *Margaret's parents want nothing to do with her because she is crippled and blind.*

- How does that make you feel?
- Do you think their reaction is: Unreasonable? Understandable? Objectionable? Justifiable? Inhuman?
- Why?

3. *Nowadays, in many countries, parents who feel this way about a disabled child can have the child killed (through abortion), even right up until birth, as almost happens to Miri.*

- Do you think this is okay?
- Why/Why not?

4. *In the same countries, disabled people usually enjoy considerable rights and protections once they are born.*

- Do you think there is an inconsistency in the way disabled people are treated in these countries?
- Why/Why not?

5. *Miri's nurse, Esme, saves his life as a baby but later refuses to adopt him.*
- How does this make you feel?
- Do you think her decision was: Perfectly acceptable? Totally unacceptable? Hideously lacking in love and generosity? Lacking in love and generosity but basically acceptable? A total failure of priorities?
- Why?

6. *In Margaret's eyes, her disabilities and sufferings were gifts from God that enabled her to draw closer to him more quickly and more effectively than she could have done without them.*
- Have you ever endured a suffering or trial, however minor, that because you managed to turn it towards God, or someone else, became in some small (or large!) way a blessing?
- If so, will you more easily turn to God in such a situation in future?
- If not, are you likely to try to offer such a suffering to God if it should occur?
- Do you think it will be easy to do?

- Why/Why not?

7. *Miri initially reacts to his accident by doubting God more than ever and growing very angry with Him. The little voice in his mind that encourages this train of thought seems very reasonable until Margaret tips him off to the possibility of the devil's influence. With this change of perspective, he grows suspicious of the 'reasonable' voice, turns his back on anger and hate, and is soon feeling happier and more positive about his life.*

- Have you ever heard arguments that seemed very reasonable on first hearing, but which later began to seem questionable?
- Did you speak to someone or read or watch something, or did something else happen, that made you see things in a different light?

8. *False arguments often seem to promise something good (truth, freedom, love, fulfillment, self-determination) yet have a corrosive effect on your life, delivering the opposite. This sort of 'anti-result' is a good indicator that the arguments come from the devil, yet it can be hard to spot and/or accept.*

- Have you ever noticed these sorts of 'anti-results' in your life or that of someone around you?
- What did you do about it?
- Did it help?

- Why/Why not?

9. *When Miri first learns that he may be dependent on a wheelchair he feels as though his life is over, that he is useless and would be better off dead. With love and support from those around him, he comes to realize that he is wrong and that his life still has just as much meaning, purpose, and potential as before—whether he can walk or only lie in bed is irrelevant. Miri comes to understand this quite quickly, but sometimes after a life-altering event it can take years or even decades for someone to reach this understanding, especially without proper support.*
   - Do you think it is ever acceptable to kill someone (through euthanasia/assisted suicide and other forms of so-called 'mercy' killing) who feels their life has no value, even if they have felt that way for some time without a change?
   - Why/Why not?

10. *Think about someone you admire greatly who is disabled or suffers from mental health problems (personal friend or family member/Paralympian/celebrity/public figure).*
   - Does thinking about all that they have achieved/all that they are change how you feel about the subject?
   - Why/Why not?

MORE INFORMATION

The Life of Blessed Margaret of Castello 1287-1320
– Fr. William R. Bonniwell
Meticulously researched but largely dramatized, this
highly readable fiction-style biography is a great
starting point for all ages.

*Blessed Margaret of Castello: Servant of the Sick and the
Outcast* – Mary Elizabeth O'Brien, OP
A detailed non-fiction biography.

Blessed Margaret of Castello: The Poor Outcast
An audio play available from:
*www.reginamartyrumproductions.com/products/poor-
outcast-blessed-margaret-castello*

Little Margaret of Castello (Movie)
The full movie is available to view on YouTube.
https://www.youtube.com/watch?v=vbKbIplfJu8

OTHER RESOURCES

www.LittleMargaret.org
Official website of the Little Margaret Guild

PRAYER TO SAINT MARGARET OF CASTELLO

O God, by whose will the blessed
virgin Margaret was blind from birth,
that the eyes of her mind being
inwardly enlightened she might think
without ceasing on You alone, be
the light of our eyes, that we may
be able to flee the shadows of this
world, and reach the home of never-
ending light. We ask this through
Christ, our Lord.

*Our Father. Hail Mary. Glory be to
the Father.*

- ✝ -

NOVENA TO SAINT MARGARET OF CASTELLO

After each day's prayer, pray the following daily prayer:
O God, by whose will the blessed virgin, Margaret,
was blind from birth, that the eyes of her mind being
inwardly enlightened she might think without
ceasing on You alone; be the light of our eyes, that we
may be able to flee the shadows of this world, and
reach the home of never ending light. We ask this
through Christ, Our Lord. Amen.

Jesus, Mary, Joseph, glorify your servant Saint Margaret, by granting the favor we so ardently desire. This we ask in humble submission to God's will, for His honor and glory and the salvation of souls.

Followed by:
one Our Father, Hail Mary, and Glory be to the Father.

DAY 1

O Saint Margaret of Castello, in embracing your life just as it was, you gave us an example of resignation to the will of God. In so accepting God's will, you knew that you would grow in virtue, glorify God, save your own soul and help the souls of your neighbors. Obtain for me the grace to recognize the will of God in all that may happen to me in my life and so resign myself to it. Obtain for me also the special favor which I now ask through your intercession with God.

Say the daily prayer, then one Our Father, Hail Mary and Glory be to the Father.

DAY 2

O Saint Margaret of Castello, in reflecting so deeply upon the sufferings and death of our Crucified Lord, you learned courage and gained the grace to bear your own afflictions. Obtain for me the grace and courage that I so urgently need so as to be able to bear my infirmities and endure my afflictions in union with our suffering Savior. Obtain for me also the special favor which I now ask through your intercession with God.

Say the daily prayer, then one Our Father, Hail Mary and Glory be to the Father.

DAY 3

O Saint Margaret of Castello, your love for Jesus in the Blessed Sacrament was intense and enduring. It was here in intimacy with the Divine Presence that you found the spiritual strength to accept sufferings, to be cheerful, patient, and kindly towards others. Obtain for me the grace that I may draw from this same source, as from an inexhaustible font, the strength whereby I may be kind and understanding of everyone despite whatever pain or discomfort may come my way. Obtain for me also the special favor which I now ask through your intercession with God.

Say the daily prayer, then one Our Father, Hail Mary and Glory be to the Father.

DAY 4

O Saint Margaret of Castello, you unceasingly turned to God in prayer with confidence and trust in His fatherly love. It was only through continual prayer that you were enabled to accept your misfortunes, to be serene, patient and at peace. Obtain for me the grace to persevere in my prayer, confident that God will give me the help to carry whatever cross comes into my life. Obtain for me also the special favor which I now ask through your intercession with God.

Say the daily prayer, then one Our Father, Hail Mary and Glory be to the Father.

DAY 5

O Saint Margaret of Castello, in imitation of the Child Jesus, who was subject to Mary and Joseph, you obeyed your father and mother, overlooking their unnatural harshness. Obtain for me that same attitude of obedience toward all those who have legitimate authority over me, most especially toward the Holy Roman Catholic Church. Obtain for me also the special favor which I now ask through your intercession with God.

Say the daily prayer, then one Our Father, Hail Mary and Glory be to the Father.

DAY 6

Oh Saint Margaret of Castello, your miseries taught you better than any teacher the weakness and frailty of human nature. Obtain for me the grace to recognize my human limitations and to acknowledge my utter dependence upon God. Acquire for me that abandonment which leaves me completely at the mercy of God to do with me whatsoever He wills. Obtain for

me also the special favor which I now ask through your
intercession with God.

Say the daily prayer, then one Our Father, Hail Mary and
Glory be to the Father.

DAY 7

O Saint Margaret of Castello, you could have so easily
became discouraged and bitter; but, instead, you fixed
your eyes on the suffering Christ and there you learned
from Him the redemptive value of suffering: how to
offer your pains and aches, in reparation for sin and for
the salvation of souls. Obtain for me the grace to learn
how to endure my sufferings with patience. Obtain for
me also the special favor which I now ask through your
intercession with God.

Say the daily prayer, then one Our Father, Hail Mary and
Glory be to the Father.

DAY 8

O Saint Margaret of Castello, how it must have hurt
when your parents abandoned you! Yet you learned
from this that all earthly love and affection, even for
those who are closest, must be sanctified. And so,
despite everything, you continued to love your parents,
but now you loved them in God. Obtain for me the
grace that I might see all my human loves and affections
in their proper perspective...in God and for God.

Obtain for me also the special favor which I now ask
through your intercession with God.
*Say the daily prayer, then one Our Father, Hail Mary and
Glory be to the Father.*

DAY 9

O Saint Margaret of Castello, through your suffering
and misfortune, you became sensitive to the sufferings
of others. Your heart reached out to everyone in trouble:
the sick, the hungry, the dying, prisoners. Obtain for me
the grace to recognize Jesus in everyone with whom I
come into contact, especially in the poor, the wretched,
the unwanted! Obtain for me also the special favor
which I now ask through your intercession with God.
*Say the daily prayer, then one Our Father, Hail Mary and
Glory be to the Father.*

CONCLUDING PRAYER

O my God, I thank you for having given Saint
Margaret of Castello to the world as an example of the
degree of holiness that can be attained by anyone who
truly loves you, regardless of physical abnormalities.
In today's secular culture, Margaret would have, most
likely, never been born; death through abortion being
seen as preferable to life, especially life in an ugly,
distorted, twisted body. But your ways are not the
world's ways…and so it was your will that Margaret

would be born into the world with just such a malformed body.

It is your way that uses our weakness to give testimony to your power. Margaret was born blind, so as to see you more clearly; a cripple, so as to lean on you completely; dwarfed in physical posture, so as to become a giant in the spiritual order; hunched-backed, so as to more perfectly resemble the twisted, crucified body of your Son. Margaret's whole life was an enactment of the words expressed by Paul:

So I shall be happy to make my weaknesses my special boast so that the power of Christ may stay over me and that is why I am content with my weaknesses, and with insults, hardships, persecutions and the agonies I go through for Christ's sake. For it is when I am weak that I am strong. (2 Cor. 12:10).

I beseech you, O God, to grant, through the intercession of Saint Margaret of Castello, that all the handicapped…and who among us is not?…all the rejected, all the UNWANTED of this world may make their weaknesses their own special boast so that your power may stay over them now and forever. Amen.

Saint Margaret of Castello, pray for us!

Say three Our Fathers and three Hail Marys.

Old Men Don't Walk to Egypt

CHAPTER 1 - MONDAY

"Hey, Katie." Shaun's eyes flick up and down me as I stop beside him in the quiet corridor, and he smiles, his arm slipping around my shoulders possessively. The ear loops of his face mask show from one trouser pocket and I slip mine off as well.

Everyone else is still in the cafeteria, eating, but with the Covid rules about class 'bubbles' this is the only time Shaun and I can meet. Even after two weeks I can still hardly believe that he actually wants me for his girlfriend! I mean, he's gorgeous, he's a fantastic rugby player, and he's several years older than me!

"Did you hear about the flash woodworking competition?" I ask him. Woodworking's not really my thing, but I have such a good idea. I'm bursting to tell him.

"Yep." He runs a hand through his hair, tousling it in a way that really suits him. "We won't be able to hang out in the park much this week; I've got to make the winning entry."

We only have one week to make our pieces and submit them. Deadline is next Monday. It's open to all four of the oldest year groups.

"I was, uh, I was thinking of entering too."

He raises his eyes from the region of my chest to glance at my face. "You?"

"Yeah. I have this fantastic idea. I know I'm not that great at woodworking but I thought maybe you could"—at the way he's frowning I swallow 'help a little' and finish lamely— "give me a few pointers?"

He's really scowling now. "Katie, I just told you I'm entering. Why would you put me in such an awkward position? Asking me to help you? That would just be silly."

"I didn't mean..." I speak quickly, my heart pounding. "I mean, I'm so..." *So rubbish at woodwork that even with your help I'm hardly going to be competition and I am your girlfriend...* But I shut up. "No, you're right. It was silly. Forget it."

He slides his arm down to my waist, lowering his head to nuzzle my cheek, but hurt and uncertainty still slosh in my stomach. I pull my phone out and ease away from him to get enough elbow room to check it.

"Why do you always do that?" His voice is sharp.

"Do what?"

"Pull away and check your phone?"

"I...I thought I heard a text alert." It's a lie, but he's looking so angry and hurt. Yet he's always checking his own phone, even if I'm speaking.

"Whatever."

I start to put the phone away but he pulls me right against him and I've drawn back before I can think. Trying to cover it up, I raise my phone again, but he grabs my wrist.

"Why don't you just put that thing away?"

"Ow! Shaun!"

"Why don't *you* get your hands off her?" The quiet voice speaks from only feet away and we both spin around. Surely I'm not *hoping* for a teacher? We're both maskless and in violation of the bubble rule...

...Aw, heck. Worse. It's a boy from my year, Daniel—bald and gaunt and pale-faced. I barely know him. When I arrived at the beginning of the school year he seemed like a quiet, slightly nerdy boy who stuck with his group of friends and didn't make any waves, but then about half-way through the term he started getting in bully's faces like he had a death wish, then he disappeared—having chemo, apparently. Some of the meaner kids were betting on whether he was going to die. He reappeared during the brief period schools were open after Christmas—bald and skeletal—then during the spring Lockdown there were rumors he was having more chemo. And now he's back again. Still bald, so I guess the rumors were correct.

Alive, though. And apparently still with a death wish, if he's getting in the face of my eighteen-year-old rugby player boyfriend.

"What did you say?" Shaun demands.

"You shouldn't be grabbing her like that."

"She's *my* girlfriend, baldie." Shaun towers over skinny Daniel, who just stares up at him, unmoved. Guess anyone who beats up the kid with leukemia will probably get expelled and he knows it.

"All the more reason," he says calmly.

Shaun looks like he's about to flatten Daniel, expulsion or not, so I say quickly, "Why are you interfering, Daniel? Shaun wasn't doing anything."

"Do you know this sack of bones?" demands Shaun. "Isn't this the Jesus-freak with cancer?"

"He's in my year, that's—" But before I can say 'all' Shaun's spun around and marched off.

"Thanks for nothing," I snap at Daniel.

"You're welcome," he says dryly.

"Freak!"

He shrugs. I pull out my mask and turn to go.

"Oh, Katie."

"What?"

"How are you doing with Mrs. Gunnings' saint research project?"

"Haven't even chosen a saint yet…." Just in time, I bite off, 'not that it's any of your business.' I mean, he's into that sort of thing, right? If he has to butt in like this, he can at least help me. "Got any tips?"

"Saint Joseph would be a good one, I reckon."

"Right." If he thinks Saint Joseph's easy to research, that'll do for me.

I head a few steps down the corridor, but pause when I see Daniel's handsome friend Razim striding towards us. Taller and broader-shouldered than Daniel, his skin is a warm brown shade, although—alas—gone is the glossy black hair with the adorable wave. He shaved it off a couple of weeks ago in some mad act of solidarity with Daniel. His older brother didn't know he'd done it until he saw him in school and they had a fight right there in the cafeteria. Seemed an overreaction on his brother's part. Much as I mourn the hair, it was a sweet thing to do.

Razim is nice-looking, even without it. I think he's quite good at football. But he doesn't seem to know I exist and, anyway, Shaun's even more handsome. And on the rugby team. And older. My friends just can't believe I'm Shaun's girlfriend, any more than I can.

Razim's vague nod towards me acknowledges that we're in the same year group, but he doesn't seem to realize I was just talking to Daniel because he goes straight up to him without looking at me again.

"Why are you hauling that around yourself, man?" Razim snags the rucksack from Daniel's shoulder and swings it onto his own back. "You'll wear yourself out and then your mum will make you stay home. Come and sit down. Where did you go, anyway?"

"I just wanted to check something out."

I think from the way his eyes crinkle above his mask that Daniel smiles at me, then he allows his friend to herd him away.

I stare after him. Check something out? Did he follow me? Why would he do that?

Ignoring the little voice that says Daniel was nearby when Shaun shouted—that is, raised his voice a bit—last week, I slip my mask on and rub my wrist. Shaun doesn't know his own strength, that's all. Daniel should keep his nose out of other people's business.

**AVAILABLE NOW
in paperback and eBook!**

I AM MARGARET SNEAK PEEK

We filed into the gym when it was all over, sitting on benches along the wall. Bane guided Jonathan Revan to a free spot over on the boys' side. In the hall through the double doors the rest of the school fidgeted and chatted. Once the end of semester assembly was over, they were free for four whole weeks.

Free. Would I ever be free again?

I'd soon know. One of the inspectors was wedging the doors open as the headmaster took his place on the stage. His voice echoed into the gym. "And now we must congratulate our New Adults! Put your hands together, everyone!"

Dutiful clapping from the hall. Doctor Vidran stood by the door, clipboard in hand, and began to read names. A boy. A girl. A boy. A girl. Sorry, a young man, a young woman. Each New Adult got up and went through to take their seat in the hall. Was there a pattern...? No, randomized. Impossible to know if they'd passed your name or not.

My stomach churned wildly now. Swallowing hard, I stared across the gym at Bane. Jonathan sat beside him, looking cool as a cucumber, if a little determinedly so. *He* wasn't in any suspense. Bane stared back at me, his face grim and his eyes fierce. I drank in the harsh lines of his face, trying to carve every beloved detail into my mind.

"They might call my name," Caroline was whispering to Harriet. "They might. It's still possible. Still possible..."

Over half the class had gone through.

Still possible, still possible, they might, they might call my name... My mind took up Caroline's litany, and

168

my desperate longing came close to an *ache*.

"Blake Marsden."

A knot of anxiety inside me loosened abruptly—immediately replaced by a more selfish pain. Bane glared at Doctor Vidran and didn't move from his seat. Red-faced, the deputy headmistress murmured in Doctor Vidran's ear.

Doctor Vidran looked exasperated. "Blake Marsden, known as Bane Marsden."

Clearly the best Bane was going to get. He gripped Jonathan's shoulder and muttered something, probably *bye*. Jonathan found Bane's hand and squeezed and said something back. Something like *thanks for everything*.

Bane shrugged this off and got up as the impatient inspectors approached him. *No...don't go, please...* Yes! He was heading straight for me—but the inspectors cut him off.

"Come on...Bane, is it? *Congratulations*, through you go..." Bane resisted being herded and the inspector's voice took on a definite warning note. "Now, you're an adult, it's your big day, don't spoil it."

"I just want to speak to..."

They caught his arms. He wrenched, trying to pull free, but they were strong men and there were two of them.

"You *know* no contact is allowed at this point. I'm sure your girlfriend will be through in a moment."

"Fiancée," snarled Bane, and warmth exploded in my stomach, chasing a little of the chill fear from my body. He'd read my story already.

"*If*, of course, your *fiancée*," Doctor Vidran sneered the un-PC word from over by the door, "is a perfect specimen. If not, you're better off without her, *aren't* you?"

Bane's nostrils flared, his jaw went rigid and his

knuckles clenched until I thought his bones would pop from his skin. Shoulders shaking, he allowed the inspectors to bundle him across the gym towards Doctor Vidran. *Uh oh...*

But by the time they reached the doors he'd got sufficient hold of himself he just stopped and looked back at me instead of driving his fist into Doctor Vidran's smug face. He seemed a long way away. But he'd never been going to reach me, had he?

"Love you..." he mouthed.

"Love you..." I mouthed back, my throat too tight for actual words.

Then a third inspector joined the other two and they shoved him through into the hall. And he was gone.

Gone. I might never see him again. I swallowed hard and clenched my fists, fighting a foolish frantic urge to rush across the gym after him.

"*Really,*" one inspector was tutting, "we don't usually have to drag them *that* way!"

"Going to end up on a gurney, that one," apologized the deputy headmistress, "So sorry about that..."

Doctor Vidran dismissed Bane with a wave of his pen and went on with the list.

"They might..." whispered Caroline, "they might..."

They might...they might...I might be joining Bane. I might... Please...

But they didn't. Doctor Vidran stopped reading, straightened the pages on his clipboard and glanced at the other inspectors. "Take them away," he ordered.

AVAILABLE NOW

in paperback and eBook!

ACKNOWLEDGEMENTS

I'd like to thank Christina Chase, Clare McCullough, Susan Peek, Barb Szyszkiewicz, and Cynthia Toney, for all their excellent editorial help, and Sr. M. Catherine Bloom, OP, for the beautiful cover illustration.

Thanks to my parents for all their support, and to my Mum for her honest critiques.

And I must not forget Saint Margaret of Castello, the patron of this book—and last but the opposite of least, the Holy Spirit, who is responsible for it all.

ABOUT THE AUTHOR

Corinna Turner has been writing since she was fourteen and likes strong protagonists with plenty of integrity. Although she spends as much time as possible writing, she cannot keep up with the flow of ideas, for which she offers thanks—and occasional grumbles!—to the Holy Spirit. She is the author of over twenty-five books, including the Carnegie Medal Nominated I Am Margaret series, and her work has been translated into four languages. She was awarded the St. Katherine Drexel award in 2022.

She is a Lay Dominican with an MA in English from Oxford University and lives in the UK. She is a member of a number of organizations, including the Society of Authors, Catholic Teen Books, Catholic Reads, the Angelic Warfare Confraternity, and the Sodality of the Blessed Sacrament. She used to have a Giant African Land Snail, Peter, with a 6½" long shell, but now makes do with a cactus and a campervan.

Sign up for **free short stories** & **news** at:
www.UnSeenBooks.com

All Free/Exclusive content subject to availability.

www.ingramcontent.com/pod-product-compliance
Lightning Source LLC
Chambersburg PA
CBHW030801190726
48285CB00003B/965

* 9 7 8 1 9 1 0 8 0 6 2 6 5 *